TH...
FOR RAIDER TO FOLLOW . . .

When Raider rode into town, he was mounted on his second horse; his big black was getting close to worn out. He felt dejected. Just a couple of days earlier he'd been certain he was going to catch up to Hill. Now he didn't have the slightest idea in which direction the bastard was headed.

His dejection made him careless, took his mind from his surroundings. He was swinging down from his horse, looking around for a telegraph office, when three men abruptly stepped out of what looked like a hotel, about forty yards away.

Raider froze. It was Hill and his two men. They froze just as still; he could see Hill turn white. And then both Raider and the three men he'd vowed to kill exploded into action . . .

Other books in the *RAIDER* series by
J. D. HARDIN

RAIDER
SIXGUN CIRCUS
THE YUMA ROUNDUP
THE GUNS OF EL DORADO
THIRST FOR VENGEANCE
DEATH'S DEAL
VENGEANCE RIDE
CHEYENNE FRAUD
THE GULF PIRATES
TIMBER WAR
SILVER CITY AMBUSH
THE NORTHWEST RAILROAD WAR
THE MADMAN'S BLADE
WOLF CREEK FEUD
BAJA DIABLO
STAGECOACH RANSOM
RIVERBOAT GOLD
WILDERNESS MANHUNT
SINS OF THE GUNSLINGER
BLACK HILLS TRACKDOWN
GUNFIGHTER'S SHOWDOWN
THE ANDERSON VALLEY SHOOT-OUT
BADLANDS PATROL
THE YELLOWSTONE THIEVES
THE ARKANSAS HELLRIDER
BORDER WAR
THE EAST TEXAS DECEPTION
DEADLY AVENGERS
HIGHWAY OF DEATH
THE PINKERTON KILLERS
TOMBSTONE TERRITORY
MEXICAN SHOWDOWN
THE CALIFORNIA KID
BORDER LAW
HANGMAN'S LAW

RAIDER

FAST DEATH

J.D. HARDIN

B

BERKLEY BOOKS, NEW YORK

FAST DEATH

A Berkley Book/published by arrangement with
the author

PRINTING HISTORY
Berkley edition / June 1990

ISBN: 0-425-12138-0

PRINTED IN THE UNITED STATES OF AMERICA

10 9 8 7 6 5 4 3 2 1

FAST DEATH

CHAPTER ONE

Raider sat with his back to the wall, but with his chair clear of it, so that he could shove the chair away from the table if he needed to move quickly.

An old buffalo hunter was dealing five card draw. The cards whispered across the scarred and stained tabletop. Raider picked up his cards, fanned them out. Two kings and a lot of junk. He looked up from his hand, studying his four opponents. One looked disgusted, but a couple of others were studying their cards with considerable interest.

Glancing past the players, Raider studied the room. It was big, bare, and ugly, with plank walls, a splintery wooden floor, a long, scarred bar, and, here and there, close to the walls, rickety tables like the one he was sitting at. Most of the floor was bare, so that the cowboys who crowded the bar could dance with the girls.

He'd counted four girls so far. They were what the newspapers liked to call "soiled doves." One was kind of pretty. Way at the back of the room small booths had been curtained off, a private place for the girls to take their cowboys, if they

1

had enough money to pay for more than dancing. From time to time, when the raucous noise that filled the place—the shouts, the singing, the bawling for more rotgut—died down a little, grunts and giggles could be heard from the other side of those curtains.

"I'm out."

Raider flicked his eyes back to the table. The player who'd looked unhappy was throwing in his cards. A dumb move; nobody had even opened yet. If he'd held, maybe everyone else would have folded.

One man, a drummer who appeared to be down on his luck, took three cards. The man directly opposite took two. Raider took three. The old buffalo hunter also took three.

Raider looked at his hand again. He'd drawn a king; he now had three of them. When it was time to bet, he checked. So did the drummer. The man opposite opened. Raider thought he detected a faint gleam of excitement in his eyes. He'd drawn only two cards so he probably had at least three of a kind. Better than three kings? Three aces, maybe?

The buffalo hunter called, unenthusiastically. Raider was about to open his mouth, when loud, angry words from the bar caused the men opposite him to turn around.

Two young cowhands were standing at the bar, about four feet apart. From their dirty, unshaven, ragged appearance, they'd just come in from a long time on the trail. "Goddamn it, Tom," one of them shouted at the other. "I tole you never ta talk 'bout that agin."

"Lookee here, Luke," the other shouted back, his Texas twang slurred by alcohol. "I'm a free man. I say what's on my mind."

"But it's a lie!"

"You callin' me a liar?"

Raider rapped on the table with the edge of his cards. "Ten dollars more," he said, having to raise his voice a little so that he could be heard over the shouting of the two cowboys.

The drummer jerked his eyes back to his cards, then glanced over his shoulder again as the two cowboys continued their shouting match. "Are you in?" Raider asked acidly.

"Uh—no."

The drummer tossed in his cards. The man opposite Raider studied his cards for a moment, hesitated, then raised another ten dollars.

Meanwhile, at the bar, the two cowboys were growing more bitter, more personal, as they shouted at one another. Others in the bar began to pull away from them. Both cowboys were packing guns; one had an old cap and ball pistol stuck into his belt, the other had what appeared to be a new Colt Peacemaker riding in a battered old holster that covered all but the tip of the butt.

"I fold," the buffalo hunter said, fanning his cards down onto the tabletop.

Now only Raider and the man opposite him remained in the game. Raider's opponent appeared to be a townie, maybe a clerk in a store. What the hell are you doing in a place like this, mister? Raider wondered. He studied the man's face. He looked nervous. Was it because of the impending fight behind him? Or did he have only three of a kind after all, and was worried that Raider might have a full house?

"I call," Raider said, sliding another ten dollar gold piece out onto the tabletop.

The townie swallowed, then laid down his cards. "Three tens," he muttered.

Then all hell broke loose. "Your old man's a lyin', two-faced horse thief!" the cowboy named Luke screamed.

Everyone in the room knew that a verbal boundary had been crossed. Everyone turned, including the townie who'd just laid down his three tens. Tom, the other cowboy, had turned white as a sheet. "Why—why you—"

He clawed for his gun, but the all-enveloping holster, plus the alcohol inside him, slowed his draw. Luke hesitated. Then, as Tom began to work the pistol out of his holster, he jerked the old cap and ball from his belt.

People were scrambling for cover even before the first shot rang out. All the players at the card table left their chairs and hit the floor, with the exception of Raider and the old buffalo hunter. By now, Tom and Luke had backed away from one another; they were standing about eight feet apart. They fired almost simultaneously. Both shots missed. Raider heard a woman scream from the rear of the saloon, as a ball from Luke's pistol whipped through a curtain screening off one of the cubicles. He caught a glimpse of white flesh. Lots of it.

The roar of gunfire was continuous, as each cowboy emptied his pistol. Raider noticed when Luke's old cap and ball misfired on the second shot. Both cowboys were so rattled that every one of their shots missed—until Luke's last shot took Tom right in the middle of the chest, over his heart.

By now the entire center of the big barroom was wreathed in a blue-white cloud of gun smoke. Still, Raider could see Tom, his pistol having fallen from his hand, sliding down the front of the bar, until his hip hit the footrail. He grabbed ineffectually at the rail, then slumped onto the floor.

Now that the shooting was obviously over, heads began to rise. Raider waited until the townie had gotten to his knees. "Three kings," Raider said calmly—it was deathly quiet in the room—and fanned out his cards.

He was raking in the money when the old buffalo hunter spoke. "You act real cool around shootin' scrapes, mister. Ever'body else hit the floor."

Raider looked the old-timer straight in the eye. "'Cept you."

The buffalo hunter shrugged. "Hell, sonny. I'm too old to go crawlin' around on floors. My knees won't take it anymore. But you—?"

Answering the old man's raised eyebrows, Raider looked down at the splintered floor, at the gobs of spat-out tobacco juice, and the horse shit that had been tracked in from the street. A slimy coating. "I just bought a new jacket."

The old man guffawed, but his laughter was cut off by an anguished cry from the direction of the bar. Luke, the winner of the gunfight, was still standing in the same place from where he'd fired his last shot. He stared at the smoking pistol in his hand, then down at Tom's sprawled body. "Tom?" he called out. "You okay, Tom?"

"Well, he sure as hell ain't feelin' no pain," someone snickered. Luke shot a wild look in the man's direction. The snicker died away. "Tom?" Luke said again, this time in a lower voice. "Oh, Tom—"

Luke dropped his pistol and went over to kneel next to Tom's lifeless body. Raider got up from his chair, stuck his winnings into his pocket, and headed for the front door. He was just stepping out onto the boardwalk, when, from behind him, he heard Luke's anguished voice. ''Oh, Tom— What am I gonna tell your ma?''

CHAPTER TWO

As he left the saloon's doorway, Raider instinctively looked both ways, alert for surprises; a man half-hidden, holding a gun, someone on a roof across the street, aiming a rifle. There was nothing, just the railroad tracks directly across from him, and beyond the tracks, Dodge City's Front Street, lined on the opposite side by a number of wooden, false-front buildings.

Raider headed for the eastern end of town with no apparent destination in mind, just walking, working the stiffness out of muscles that had spent too many hours sitting in a chair.

He could smell them before he reached them: the stock pens, Dodge City's reason for existence. A herd had come in the day before; the pens were jammed with bawling, milling longhorn cattle, up from Texas, waiting to be jammed into railroad cars and shipped north and east, to the enormous packing houses in Chicago, Saint Louis, and Philadelphia.

Raider leaned against a fence, watching tired-looking, dirty cowboys prodding cattle with long poles, forcing them up a narrow chute into a cattle car. Punchers. People were starting to call the trailhands cowpunchers, cowpokes, because of this highly visible work with the poles. The cowboys didn't like either name at all; this was one of their least favorite jobs.

The dust began to annoy Raider. He turned and walked back into town. He'd gone only a few yards when he heard the thunder of hooves behind him, mixed with high-pitched yells. He spun around, then relaxed when he saw that it was only a group of three cowboys, freshly released from work at the pens, riding hell-bent for the sin parlors of Dodge City. One pulled out an old cap and ball pistol and blew off several shots into the air.

Raider noticed three people across the street, flattening themselves against a wall. They were obviously a family; a man, a woman, and a boy about eight or nine years old. Raider saw the look of contempt, even hatred, the woman was giving the three celebrating cowhands. Sodbuster, Raider thought. No—townie. Straitlaced, Methodist townies, aghast at the sin and corruption that flourished in places like the saloon from which he'd just come. The saloon in which a young cowboy named Tom lay dead.

The family, which had been heading toward the stock pens, quickly reversed its course and started back toward the center of town. They were on the north side of the street, opposite Raider, heading in the same direction. He saw the woman turn her head and look at the collection of ramshackle buildings that lay south of the railroad tracks. The sporting district, an area designated by the town fathers as wide open to any vice, riddled, in the woman's eyes, by sin. Blackest sin.

Raider saw the disgust on her face, saw it deepen into horror when the door of a small house opened to let out a man. Behind him, a naked woman stepped into the doorway, half out into the open, and ran her right hand affectionately through the man's hair. The woman on the street abruptly reached down and turned her son's face away. "Jezebel!" she hissed, glaring at the nude woman. Raider grinned. He had already noticed the boy's wide-eyed fascination, and the reluctance with which he turned his head.

Bleeding Kansas. The phrase popped into Raider's mind. He'd first heard those words when he was a boy, on the hard-scrabble Arkansas farm where he'd grown up. Bleeding Kansas, a battleground between pro- and anti-slavery forces back in the fifties, battling to determine Kansas's future—slave or free. Then, during the war, terrible butchery had been inflicted on this unhappy land by Confederate guerrilla groups, who wiped out entire towns; men, women, and children.

And now, there was another invasion, of Texas cattle and Texas cowboys, bringing both scourge and blessing to Kansas: the men with money to spend, but full of the usual Texas violence; the longhorns, gold on the hoof, but carrying in and on their bodies Texas cattle diseases that threatened local stock.

All those longhorns, left to multiply unmolested while Texas men were off fighting the war. Raider remembered what one old-timer Texan had said: "Damn it all! If we'd o' got back any later, the whole southern part o' the state woulda sunk under the weight o' them cows."

Millions of cattle, no market. Then the railroads had begun to push west into Kansas, due north of the West Texas plains. Railroads that ran to the huge packing houses in the north. Texas cattlemen like Charles Goodnight, cattle-rich, but cash-poor, had seen the potential, and within four years after the end of the war, herds were already pushing north, on the three-month run to the Kansas railhead towns. First Abilene; then Wichita and Newton; now, Dodge City.

Raider had been through Dodge several years before, when it was a mere adjunct of nearby Fort Dodge, just a collection of log buildings and lean-tos. Sure has changed a lot, he thought, as he glanced at all the new buildings, already aging under the punishing weather of the Kansas plains. Front Street widened in the center of town, north of the tracks, an area known as the plaza, and on its north side were the establishments that sucked money out of cowboy pockets and into the pockets of Dodge citizens such as that disapproving family: the Iowa Hotel, the Long Branch Saloon, the Dodge House, Delmonico's Restaurant, the Alhambra; the big stores, waiting patiently through the winter for the first herds of the year. After months on the trail, eating cow dust, Dodge City was the cowboy's dream. Babylon on the plains.

And the source of a peculiar Kansas schizophrenia; a lust for what the cowboy had in his pockets, warring against Methodist prudery. Raider noticed the fine clothing the members of that little family were wearing. They'd obviously made their pile off the cowboy invasion. Yet they clearly hated the cowboys, even the father. He scowled in the direction from which Raider had come, the sporting district, south of the tracks. Hypocrites. The hypocrisy of the righteous, something Raider particularly despised.

He crossed the tracks, heading toward the Long Branch. He had to pass close to the family. The woman had found a new focus for her disgust; a cowboy reeling down the street, desperately clutching a half-full bottle of rotgut whiskey. "Demon rum," he heard the woman hiss to her husband. "Someday we'll get rid of it here in Kansas. We'll outlaw it. We'll make Kansas safe for God-fearing people."

"Amen," her husband muttered automatically. Raider watched as they entered a store, apparently their own. As they opened the door, Raider could see whiskey stocking several shelves. The hypocrisy of greed. He shuddered, and pushed his way into the Long Branch. Better get a drink before somebody did outlaw it.

The Long Branch was a considerably more elegant establishment than the dive which Raider had just left. Mirrors behind the bar made the room seem much larger. The bar was less scarred, the furniture generally unbroken. As usual, when he entered the Long Branch, his eyes lifted to a huge painting that decorated one of the walls: a nude woman, lying on a silken bed, a gauzy sheet hiding nothing of her voluptuous body. Her bed was being pulled along on a strange, flat, airborne wagon, drawn through a turbulent sky of greenish storm clouds by black and white snorting steeds. The painting was labeled, appropriately, "The Cowboy's Dream." Raider nodded. He had always experienced a strong desire to meet the model who'd inspired this particular chunk of high art.

His attention shifted from the painting to the Long Branch's patrons. There were few people at the bar; most were seated at the gambling tables near the back of the room. Luke Short, who held the saloon's gambling concession, was dealing. Raider's eyes narrowed a little as he recognized one of the other players, Wyatt Earp, a town marshal. Raider had never particularly cared for Earp; he considered him a bully, too quick to slam the barrel of his Colt up against the head of a celebrating cowboy. He had been run out of Wichita only a year or two ago for beating up a local politician.

He was effective, though. There were few hell-raisers who cared to buck Wyatt Earp. Since he'd arrived in Dodge, violence had declined considerably.

Bat Masterson was seated next to Earp. A good-looking kid, Raider thought. Maybe only twenty-one, twenty-two years old, but he'd already made a name for himself; first, at the Adobe Wells fight a couple of years back, where he'd been one of fifty buffalo hunters who'd held off five hundred Comanches for days, killing a large number of them. Then, not long ago, he'd killed a gunman, an army sergeant, in a fight over the favors of a dance hall girl. Bat had taken a bullet in that fight, but had survived it. The girl did not; she'd been killed by the sergeant's first bullet.

Raider liked Bat. Everyone seemed to like him. He, the same as Earp, was a town marshal, and always ready to back up Wyatt. The two men were close friends.

Raider leaned against the bar, trying to decide whether or not to enter the game. Formidable opponents, all of them. Like so many Western lawmen, the Dodge City marshals supplemented their pay by gambling. He'd heard that Earp was trying to buy the gambling concession at one of the smaller saloons. Raider smiled, wondering what the average Eastern city-dweller would think if he had to run to a saloon to fetch the local law.

Raider was still trying to decide whether or not to enter the game when he became aware of several men passing by on the boardwalk. Their route took them directly past the saloon's open doors, not far from where Raider was standing.

He forced himself not to turn his head too quickly. Instead, he watched the passing men out of the corner of his eye. He paid particular attention to a tall, well-dressed, clean-shaven man in the center of the group. Damned it it wasn't Benjamin Hill, the man whose presence had brought Raider to Dodge City.

CHAPTER THREE

The bartender was looking inquiringly at Raider. Raider shook his head and headed for the door. When he stepped out onto the boardwalk, Hill and the men with him were already about fifty feet away. Instead of following, Raider walked in the opposite direction. There was no need to trail after them. Dodge was small; he would have no trouble seeing where they went.

Lounging against a doorframe, Raider watched Hill and the other men go into a building near the far end of town. The sign over the building indicated that it was a saloon. After waiting a few minutes, Raider raider walked straight to the saloon the others had entered. When he pushed his way in through the swinging doors, he found himself in an establishment considerably less elegant than the Long Branch. It bore more of a resemblance to the place where Raider had been gambling earlier, although it was not quite as dirty.

And, unlike the other saloon, which lay on the wild and woolly side of the deadline, there were no guns in evidence. A town law prohibited guns north of the railroad tracks. A man could carry a gun into town, but had to immediately deposit it at a saloon or hotel, then pick it up again on his way out of town. Both of Raider's rifles, plus his big Colt Peacemaker were stashed at his hotel. But not the brand-new Colt Sheriff's Model he had recently bought, with the cut-down barrel. It was thrust into the rear waistband of his trousers, under his coat. Raider did not feel comfortable unarmed.

Hill was seated at a table near the rear of the room, with several other men. He looked straight at Raider when he came in, studied him for a moment—just a moment longer than Raider found comfortable—then looked away. Raider moved to the bar and ordered a beer.

Now it was his turn to study Hill and the men with him. Three of the men appeared to be Mexicans, although they looked subtly different than most Mexicans Raider has seen. He was aware that one of the men was talking in Spanish to Hill. One of the others cut in with another quick spate of Spanish.

Raider was close enough to hear most of the conversation. He understood Spanish well enough to realize that the men were indeed not Mexicans; their accent was different. They were not saying much of importance, merely talking about some horses they had just bought.

Raider returned his attention to Hill, trying not to be obvious about it. Hill was a little more than medium height, well-dressed in dark, expensive-looking clothing. His eyes were light in color, either gray or gray-blue, Raider couldn't quite tell. He was clean-shaven, and appeared to be somewhere in his middle to late forties, maybe even fifty.

Raider's attention was distracted from Hill when a man came out of a back room. He was big, impressively big, with short, spiky blond hair and brutal features. Muscles bulged across wide shoulders. His hands were like hams. He walked over to the table where Hill was sitting with the others. "Anything I can do for you, Mr. Hill?" he asked, rather ingratiatingly, in a voice that was ridiculously high for a man his size.

Hill looked up at the man. To Raider, it seemed like a very cold look; then he realized that the word cold would not adequately describe the way Hill was looking at the man. He simply looked at him without any apparent emotion, as if he were part of the furniture. "No, Rafe. Nothing at all," Hill replied.

Hill's voice was flat, noncommittal. It was a voice of dismissal. Either Rafe was not aware of the dismissal, or he chose to ignore it. "Been real quiet lately, Mr. Hill. Nothin' busted. I keep 'em in line."

Hill had started to return his gaze to the Latin men opposite him. Now his eyes swiveled back to Rafe. He studied him as if he were a bug. Rafe, despite his size, grew noticeably nervous.

Raider was wondering if Hill was going to say anything more, when suddenly the swinging doors slammed open, and a young cowboy, probably no more than seventeen or eighteen years old, came into the room. He was obviously very drunk. He stood just inside the doorway for a moment, swaying back and forth, his eyes struggling to focus. Finally, his eyes located the bar, and they lit up a little. The cowboy made a wandering path to the bar and nearly feel against it. "Bartender," the cowboy slurred, "I wanna buy a nickel's worth o' whiskey."

The bartender started to say something, then hesitated, his eyes flicking toward Hill. Raider saw Hill shake his head almost imperceptibly.

The bartender turned back to the cowboy. "We don't sell a nickel's worth of whiskey here," he finally said.

From Rafe's conversation with Hill, Raider figured that the saloon probably belonged to Hill. He'd been told that Hill owned a lot of property and businesses in the Kansas trail towns. Raider also suspected that the bartender might have sold the cowboy a nickel's worth of whiskey if Hill had not been present.

The young cowboy seemed confused for a moment. "But I on'y got a nickel," he said. Then his eyes brightened again. "Tell ya what," he slurred. "I got a buddy down the street. He'll be here in a li'l while, an' he's got more'n a dollar. Why doncha just gimme a bottle o' whiskey now, an' when he gits here, we'll pay."

"Can't do that, cowboy," the bartender said, shaking his head.

Once again the cowboy looked confused. "But—you got lotsa bottles. There's one right here."

A nearly full bottle was sitting directly behind the edge of the bar. Before the bartender could stop him, the cowboy reached over the bar and took hold of the bottle by the neck. The bartender made a grab for it, but the cowboy stepped back just out of reach. Laughing good-naturedly, the cowboy pulled the cork from the bottle and took a drink. Whiskey dribbled down his chin.

The bartender leaned over the bar and grabbed the base of the bottle. "Hey—don't!" the cowboy cried out. He tried to move farther backward, but as he moved, the bottle slipped from his unsteady grip. The bartender did his best to hang onto the bottle, but he was too far off balance. The bottle fell onto the floor and shattered.

The cowboy stepped back and stared down half-comprehendingly at the puddle of whiskey spreading out over the dirty planks next to his boots. Then he began to grow angry. "What the hell did you have to go an' do that for?" he screamed at the bartender. "I tole you my buddy would be here in a few minutes. I woulda paid for it. Now it's busted, an' damned if I'll pay a red cent."

The bartender shot an anxious look in Hill's direction. Hill looked up at Rafe. "I thought you said you had this place under control," he said quietly.

Rafe paled, then his face turned red with anger. Not anger at Hill, but anger at the cowboy. "You little shit!" he snarled, half-running toward the befuddled young man.

Raider knew that the cowboy would not have had a chance even if he'd been sober; Rafe was just too big for him, and too damned mean. A professional bouncer. He slammed his huge fist into the cowboy's face; then, as the surprised young man staggered back, blood already pouring from his crushed mouth, Rafe hit him in the ribs. The cowboy jackknifed in agony, and while he was doubled up, hands pressed to his ribs, Rafe kneed him in the face. Raider could clearly hear the cowboy's nose break.

But that did not end it. Rafe clubbed the cowboy to the floor with both fists. And even then it did not end. Rafe proceeded to kick the fallen man in the ribs. Raider could hear the cowboy, now only half-conscious, grunt each time Rafe kicked him.

Raider glanced toward Hill. For the first time he saw an emotion on the man's face. Pleasure. Cold, smirking pleasure. He was not going to stop what was happening.

Raider moved with no apparent haste, but suddenly he was standing next to Rafe. "That's enough," he said quietly. "He's finished."

He laid his hand on Rafe's arm. Rafe spun toward him instantly, his eyes wild, excited from the beating he was giving the boy. "Goddamn it, mister," he snarled. "You better learn when to mind your own business."

He drew his foot back, ready to kick the boy once again. Raider stepped on Rafe's other foot, and, grabbing the back of his shirt collar, pulled him backward and a little to one side. Rafe, standing only on one leg, which he could not move, since Raider was standing on his foot, fell. When he tried to put out an arm to catch himself, Raider took hold of the arm, twisted it behind Rafe's back and slammed him to the floor, facedown, with his face pressed against the spilled whiskey on the filthy floor. "Might be a good idea if you just stayed down there a little while, Rafe," Raider said, just as quietly as before, but there was no mistaking the menace in his voice.

Rafe was not to be subdued that easily. Howling with rage, he twisted partway around, and began to get up, despite Raider's hold on his arm. The man was incredibly strong, and seemingly impervious to pain. Raider suddenly let go of Rafe's arm, once again upsetting his balance, and before Rafe could recover, Raider hammered a short, hard blow down against the side of his jaw.

Rafe's eyes seemed to spin in every possible direction, and he went down again. But he was not quite completely out. Raider could see the big man gathering his hands beneath his body, ready to spring to his feet when he recovered his senses. Raider moved forward, ready to hammer Rafe again, but a voice cut in sharply. "That's enough!"

Raider had been aware of Hill and his entourage during every moment of his short encounter with Rafe. Out of the corner of his eyes, he'd seen the three Latins leap to their feet, but instead of moving directly toward him, they'd first looked at Hill, as

if for directions. Hill had motioned them back with a languid
wave of his hand.

Hill stood up and walked toward Raider. Raider stepped to
one side, far enough away from Rafe so that the downed man
could not grab his leg. Raider was aware of the three Latins
fanned out just behind Hill.

Raider's eyes moved over the four men, looking for weapons. He could not see any, but that did not mean they were
unarmed. He thought of his own hideout Sheriff's Special. He
could feel its hammer cutting into his back. It was shoved into
his waistband just a little to the right of his spine, with the butt
pointing to the right. To draw, he'd have to reach behind him
with his right hand, palm backward, and while he was drawing,
he stood a chance of blowing a hole in his own side if his
thumb slipped off the hammer. Not the best possible situation,
but he was still happy that the gun was there.

Hill saw the slight movement of Raider's right hand toward
his back, and he understood. "No need for that," he said.
Raider relaxed a little, but kept his hand ready. He moved a
little farther to the side, since Rafe was slowly getting up.
"Where is the son of a bitch?" Rafe muttered thickly. "I'll
kill him."

"You'll do nothing, Rafe," Hill snapped. "I already said
it's over."

"But the bastard—"

"Rafe—" Hill said softly, turning his face toward the big
man. Rafe saw the cold killing light in Hill's eyes, and he
paled. Raider noticed Hill's expression, too, and now he saw
that Hill's eyes were a cold, blue-gray, with one eye a little
darker than the other.

"I didn't mean nothin', Mr. Hill," Rafe muttered sullenly,
wiping at the whiskey and dirt that was smeared over one side
of his face.

Raider could feel the hate that Rafe was glaring in his direction, but he figured that Hill had calmed him down for the
moment. He turned back toward Hill, who was studying him
openly.

What Hill saw was a tall man, six foot two, with broad
shoulders. A powerfully built man, although not as bulky as

Rafe. He studied Raider's features. They were strong, perhaps even handsome features, with a thick black moustache setting off strong, white teeth. Raider's hair was black, too. A shock of it now hung down over his eyes.

It was the eyes that caught Hill's attention. Black eyes, showing tiny dancing sparks of light. Eyes that were wary at the moment, but eyes that showed no fear at all.

"I like the way you handle yourself," Hill finally said. "How would you like a job?"

Raider jerked his head toward Rafe, who was slowly rubbing his bruised jaw, while he stared hard at Raider. "A job like his?" Raider asked. "Not likely." He glanced at the fallen cowboy. "I think me an' you got a different way of enjoyin' life."

Hill's eyes seemed to turn a muddy gray. Raider wondered if he might be in big trouble again. Then a cowboy slammed open the swinging doors and came barging into the room. "Billy?" he called out. "Where the hell are—?"

Then he saw the boy sprawled on the floor. "Billy? For God's sake, is that you?"

He quickly went over to his friend, and knelt next to him. "What happened?" he asked, looking up at the bartender.

"Just—for God's sake get him out of here while he's still breathin'," the bartender hissed.

The cowboy looked from the bartender, to Billy, then toward the tense knot of men near the rear of the room. "Yeah," he muttered. "Sure."

As he began to haul Billy to his feet, Raider moved to help him. Together, they half-dragged the moaning boy to the door. Sensing that the cowhand had Billy under control, Raider quickly turned back to face Hill and his men. Hill looked at him steadily for a moment. "I'll remember you," Hill said flatly.

Then Hill turned toward Rafe. As Raider went out the door, he heard Hill say to Rafe, "You're fired. I don't hire men who get taken out that easily."

"But, Mr. Hill," Rafe whined. "He sucker punched me. I—"

"Shut up. Clear out your gear."

If Rafe made a reply, Raider didn't hear it. By then he was already out on the boardwalk. He rubbed the knuckles of his right hand with the palm of his left. They were a little sore from the contact they'd made with Rafe's jaw. Not a good move, Raider thought to himself. He'd managed to draw one hell of a lot of attention—right in front of the man he was supposed to be investigating. But damned if he could have let that kid take any more of a beating.

Raider headed along the boardwalk to his left, toward his hotel. He had only gone about thirty yards when he heard the swinging doors of the saloon he'd just left slam open behind him. "You son of a bitch!" a high-pitched, angry voice shouted from behind him.

Raider spun around. He immediately became aware of two things: Rafe, standing just outside the saloon doors, holding an enormous old cap and ball dragon revolver, and farther down the street, Wyatt Earp and Bat Masterson stepping out the front door of the Long Branch saloon.

Rafe was already raising the immense old horse pistol. Raider clearly heard the hammer click into full cock. He moved to the side, pulling the Sheriff's Model forty-five from behind his back. Rafe shot first, but Raider's quick movement had saved him; the bullet passed through the spot where Raider had been standing only moments before. Raider fired a split-second later, but the poor balance of the short-barreled, unfamiliar pistol threw off his aim, and he missed.

Not having seen a weapon on Raider earlier, Rafe had thought he was unarmed, but now that his supposedly easy target was shooting back, Rafe panicked. He began firing as quickly as he could crank back the hammer. His shots flew wild, breaking glass, and chipping splinters from walls and posts.

Cursing the short-barreled Sheriff's Special, Raider dropped down behind a rain barrel. Cocking the pistol, he rested it on top of the barrel and took careful aim. He heard a bullet from Rafe's pistol thud into the front of the barrel, and then his own pistol fired.

The bullet hit Rafe right in the center of his chest. The barrel of Raider's pistol's may have been short, but the bullet was still forty-five caliber, and Rafe was thrown backward by the impact, his cap and ball firing its last shot harmlessly into the air. Raider might have fired again; Rafe was still on his feet, staggering backward, but Raider was aware of Wyatt Earp racing toward him, with Masterson not far behind. There was a gun in Earp's hand.

Rafe finally fell, flat on his back, his pistol slipping from limp fingers. Raider stood up slowly, careful to keep his revolver pointed downward. Earp came to an abrupt stop about a yard away. "Give me that damned gun!" he snarled.

Earp raised his pistol threateningly, as if he were about to hit Raider on the head with it, one of his favorite tactics. "I wouldn't do that, if I was you," Raider said coolly. "Calm down an' you can have the gun." He jerked his chin toward Rafe's unmoving body. "I don't think I'm gonna need it anymore, anyhow."

Mad little lights were dancing in Earp's eyes. Raider was sure Earp was going to try to hit him with his pistol barrel, maybe even shoot him. He'd shoot back before he'd let that happen.

The tension between the two big men was broken when Masterson stepped between them. "He said he'd give you the gun, Wyatt," he said to Earp. "I saw the whole thing. That yahoo over there"—he gestured toward Rafe— "tried to shoot him in the back. He got what was coming to him."

Earp nodded reluctantly, then reached out his hand. Raider handed him his pistol, butt first, fingers clear of the trigger guard. "What the hell are you doing carrying a gun in my town?" Earp snapped at Raider.

Raider shrugged, then looked over in Rafe's direction. Rafe had not moved at all since he'd gone down. "Sure am glad I did," he said casually.

Masterson laughed. Earp shot him a quick glance, but by now he'd realized that he could not keep up his anger and also maintain his dignity. "Still against the law," he snapped to Raider. "You'll have to appear before the magistrate."

Earp turned toward Masterson, indicating by a jerk of his chin where Rafe lay. "Bat?" he asked. "Would you mind going over and seeing if that gent is still breathing?"

Masterson walked over to Rafe and looked down at him. "Looks dead as they get," he called back. "Damned fine shooting, with that cut-down forty-five. Maybe I ought to get me one."

Raider did not have a chance to find out what they did with Rafe's body. Earp insisted that he go straight before the magistrate. "Unless you want to go tomorrow," he said darkly, "and spend the night in the calaboose."

Raider had no particular desire to sample Dodge City's lockup, so he walked along with Earp and Masterson to the magistrate's office, where he was fined ten dollars for discharging a firearm within the city limits.

Earp insisted that Raider's Sheriff's Special be impounded. The magistrate agreed, and Raider watched his pistol go into a drawer. The way Earp's eyes followed the pistol as it was shut away suggested to Raider that it might end up in Earp's pocket. Or be sold by him for a little extra income. Raider cursed silently. The damned gun had cost him twenty dollars. Add to that the ten he'd been fined—

He was about to protest to the magistrate, maybe say something particularly unpleasant to Earp, when he remembered that he'd just used that same pistol to shoot his way out of a potentially fatal encounter. Well worth the thirty dollars.

CHAPTER FOUR

Raider realized that there was now no chance of working undercover; he had originally considered the option of infiltrating Hill's organization. Since the scene in the saloon with Rafe, that might be a good way to get a bullet in the back.

But perhaps open enmity was just as good an option. Perhaps having someone staring down his throat would apply pressure to Hill, cause him to make stupid moves.

So far, stupid moves had not been evident in Hill's behavior. McParland had told Raider, when giving him his orders back in Denver a few days ago, "We're pretty damn sure it's him. But he doesn't hardly ever fuck up. It's going to be hard to pin him down."

James McParland was a massive man, beginning to run a little toward fat, but still strong as an ox. He'd only recently taken over the Denver office, the far western headquarters of the Pinkerton National Detective Agency. Raider respected McParland because he'd worked his way up the ladder the hard way; he'd spent years in the field, laying his life on the line. He sure as hell wasn't any spoiled college boy, promoted because he'd got himself a fancy piece of paper. Raider had once seen McParland walk right up to an armed desperado he'd been hunting for months, tear a pistol from the man's grip, then knock him flat with one punch.

Just a week ago, Raider had sat in McParland's office, one leg crossed over the other, listening. "But you're sure that this man, Hill, is the one b'hind the robberies?" he finally asked.

McParland shrugged. "Pretty damned sure. If we were a hundred percent sure, he wouldn't still be operating. He'd be swinging at the end of a rope. You know how the Old Man feels."

Raider nodded. The Old Man. Old Allan Pinkerton, who had founded the Agency twenty years earlier. Neither the Agency, nor the Old Man, was averse to turning over to a lynch mob any man they were sure was guilty.

McParland had just spent the last half hour outlining the situation to Raider. Cattle buyers from the big packing houses in Chicago and Saint Louis, bringing cash to purchase entire herds out in the Kansas cattle towns, were being robbed. "Someone seems to know when they're carrying lots of money," McParland said. "There's all kinds of little things that point to Hill."

McParland told Raider what little he knew about Hill. "He just kind of appeared out of nowhere, back in the late sixties, a couple of years after the war ended. He already had money, not a lot, but enough cash to set himself up in the cattle shipping towns. He started in Abilene, back around sixty-eight, and that's when the robberies started. Then he moved on. You know how the railroads keep pushing the railhead farther west, first from Abilene to Wichita, then on through Newton, and now this new place, Dodge City. Well, Hill just moved along with the trade. He seems to like buying and building hotels, saloons, and sporting houses. When the rails move on, he either sells or abandons what he's got, then gets new ones farther down the line."

"You figger he uses these places t' find out who's carryin' money?"

McParland shrugged again. "Probably. The trouble is, we never really know what the son of a bitch owns. He sets up other people as fronts, then puts a bar or sporting house in their name. We could track it all down, but by the time we finish, he'd have moved on.''

''What else do you know about him?''

''Not a lot; it's all speculation, rumor. There's talk that he was connected, somehow, with Quantrill's Raiders, during the war, and later with Bloody Bill Anderson. He didn't actually ride with them, but there was some connection. Maybe he handled their intelligence work. He's smart enough, and they had quite a system.''

Raider fidgeted a little in his seat. He'd been born a Southerner, and had a natural sympathy for the Southern cause. But he did not like men like Quantrill and Anderson, who had been butchers, who had led gangs of bandits, rather than soldiers. Everyone still remembered Quantrill's raid on Lawrence, Kansas, back in sixty-three, when Quantrill's guerrilla force had invaded that unfortunate town, and slaughtered over a hundred fifty helpless, unarmed civilians. They were not the kind of men whom Raider cared to have championing any of his causes. The James boys, Jesse and Frank, had ridden with these same guerrillas. That's where they'd learned their outlaw skills, their taste for robbing and killing.

Raider asked the natural question. ''You think mebbe Hill's tied up with the James gang?''

McParland shook his head. ''Nope. Hill seems to be running his own show. And doing a damned good job of it. He's one smart hombre.''

Despite the suspicion directed at him, Hill had never openly fallen afoul of the law. ''He don't even do his own killing,'' McParland snorted. ''Hires other people, keeps his own skirts clean. Like I already said, we're pretty damned sure he's behind these robberies, but we don't have the kind of evidence against him that would hold up in court. It's gonna be your job to find that evidence.''

And now, having been in Dodge City only a couple of days, Raider was wondering if he'd already bungled the operation. Sure, he'd seen evidence to back up one part of McParland's theory. Rafe. Raider had checked. Rafe was listed as the owner of the saloon where he'd beaten up the cowhand. Yet he'd deferred to Hill, practically groveled in front of him. Rafe was obviously one of Hill's front men. But that wasn't the kind of evidence McParland had been talking about. It was only an indication, a suggestion that maybe they were onto the right man.

Raider spent the next couple of days playing cards in saloons, hanging around dance halls, and generally roaming the town, like any drifter, while listening for gossip, anything that he might hear about Hill. It was not work he enjoyed; he did not much care for towns, other than as places to find whiskey and women. He hated this sneaking around; he'd much rather be out on the open trail, running down a fugitive, or busting up a robbery. Openly. But, as the Agency constantly told its operatives—they insisted on the word operative, rather than agent—detective work, the slow, careful collection of information, was the cornerstone of good law enforcement. And if the detective work was successful, the opportunity for action would naturally follow.

Raider's aim was to make himself an established feature of the town, and thus, as invisible as possible. He roamed the streets, won at cards just a little more than he lost, not enough to attract a lot of attention, pretended to get drunk, and sometimes did not have to pretend.

What bothered him the most was not being armed. After he'd killed Rafe, the town marshals were keeping a sharp eye on him, particularly Wyatt Earp. He was a hard son of a bitch, but Raider had to admit that the marshals had their hands full with the trail crews. Drunken cowboys, eager to blow off steam after months on the trail, caused unending trouble. Most of the time it was merely high jinks, like the time an exuberant cowboy lassoed one of the town's leading citizens off his horse, " 'Cause he looked so damned serious," the cowboy explained later, in jail.

And of course, there were those who were drawn to wide-open, cash-rich towns like Dodge. Scum. Gamblers, pimps, confidence men, and just plain killers, who only felt at home in lawless settings.

There were numerous shootings, but most of them took place south of the deadline, where the no firearms provision was not enforced. South of the railroad tracks, vice flourished un-impeded. But if a cowboy left the sporting district, and packed his gun into the town itself, then the long arm of the law made short work of him.

One afternoon Raider was leaning against a post in front of a dry goods store when he saw two drunken cowhands leave a saloon over on the wrong side of the tracks. They headed across Front Street, straight for the Long Branch. One of them was packing his six-shooter, openly, complete with holster and gun belt. He had just reached the boardwalk when Wyatt Earp came striding quickly toward him. "Hand over your pistol, cowboy," Earp snapped.

The cowhand had been standing on tiptoe, craning his neck so that he could peer over the saloon's swinging doors, probably trying to see if there were any women inside. He turned, scowl-ing, obviously annoyed by the tone of the marshal's voice. "Who the hell do you think you are?" he started to say. "This here's a free—"

Perhaps his right hand drifted a little too close to the butt of his pistol. Perhaps Earp was simply doing what he liked to do. The marshal's pistol was immediately in his hand. He brought the barrel down against the cowboy's head. The cowhand's hat softened the blow, but the boy—he couldn't have been much more than eighteen—staggered, his hat falling onto the ground.

Earp backhanded him with the pistol, hitting him right over the eye. The sharp front sight of the marshal's pistol slashed a deep cut in the skin, and the boy clapped his hand to his bleeding head, howling in pain.

Earp immediately lifted the cowboy's gun from its holster, then began prodding him along, toward the jail. The cowboy's companion, after a moment's stunned silence, began to pace alongside Earp and his prisoner. "You didn't have no call to do that," he shouted. "Billy woulda give you the gun. He just don't like bein' talked to that way. You had no right to pistol whip him."

Earp turned a cold eye on the second cowboy. "You want some of the same, sonny?" he asked coldly.

The young man backed away, but he was not cowed.

"You're a big man with that gun," he said. "I wonder how big you are without it?"

The marshal had stopped walking. He turned to face the cowboy. "Would you like to find out?" he asked softly.

The cowboy shook his head. "Not me. I ain't got the size to take you. But I know a man who does."

He spun quickly and walked away, heading back toward the sporting district. Earp watched him go, then began prodding his dazed and bleeding prisoner again, directing him toward the jail.

Raider remained leaning against his post. He was not impressed by Earp's eagerness to hit young cowboys on the head. But Dodge was a rough town. Perhaps Earp felt that it was necessary to throw the fear of God into every man who might entertain the slightest notion of breaking the peace. Still—

Raider was wondering what to do next—he was getting bored as hell hanging around Dodge—when he heard a commotion coming from the other side of the deadline, a murmur of many men, punctuated by an occasional shout. A couple of minutes later a crowd of about a dozen cowhands came surging out of a saloon, heading for the main part of town. Raider noticed that several were openly packing guns. And they all looked angry as hell.

The shouting obviously carried to the jail. The men were in the middle of the wide plaza that lay in front of the Long Branch when Wyatt Earp and Bat Masterson stepped out of the marshal's office onto the boardwalk. The two men glanced at one another, then spread out, moving to stand about eight feet apart.

The crowd of cowboys walked up close to the boardwalk, every one of them glaring up at Earp. The cowboy who'd been with the man Earp had pistol-whipped stepped forward. "We ain't gonna take this no more, Earp," he snarled. "It's time you stopped hidin' behind your gun and fought like a man."

"We already had this conversation, sonny," Earp said coolly.

"Yeah," the cowboy replied, grinning. "But since then I been talkin' to the man who can take you down a peg or two."

Without further invitation, one of the cowhands stepped forward. Raider was still leaning against his post, no more than ten yards from the cowboys. A big son of a bitch, he thought. Big, young, and strong. Maybe a little stupid, too.

The cowboy moved to a position just below where Earp was standing. "You got the guts to take off those guns, Earp?" he asked, grinning insultingly up at the marshal. That's when Raider decided that he must be stupid. It was a high boardwalk. It would be an easy move for Earp to kick him straight in the face.

Instead, Earp walked to the side, then stepped down into the dust of the street, a little to the left of the cowboys, and right in front of where Raider was standing. Masterson followed, standing just behind Earp. When Earp began unbuckling his gun belt, the cowboys hooted and hollered enthusiastically. "Come on, Hiram!" they shouted to the big cowboy. "Show him some Texas style dancin'!"

By now, Earp had handed his gun belt to Masterson. Hiram, enjoying the attention, stripped off his shirt and handed it to one of the cowboys. Muscles rippled. Yes, he sure as hell is a big one, Raider thought again. Maybe six foot four, with shoulders as wide as an ox span, and heavy arms that hung down like an ape's.

Earp seemed unimpressed. While Hiram posed and strutted in front of his friends, Earp simply walked up and hit him in the mouth; a single blow, with no attempt at a follow-up. "Did you come here to fight, or to show off your tits?" Earp asked mockingly. Then he stepped back, assuming a boxing stance.

Hiram raised his hand to his mouth. It came away covered with his own blood. "Why you—" he shouted, launching himself at Earp.

For the next five minutes, Raider was treated to an impressive exhibition of pugilistic skill—on Earp's part. Hiram charged repeatedly, swinging wildly. He even connected a few times, leaving some cuts, and a big swelling over Earp's left eye, but on the whole it was the marshal's show all the way. He jabbed, slipped punches, and chopped short rights, until Hiram's face was a mask of blood and puffy flesh.

When he'd cut up the cowboy's face sufficiently, Earp began to work on his body, slamming into Hiram's ribs and belly, until the big man was grunting for breath. It was clear to everybody that Earp was only playing with Hiram, that he could end it any time he wanted. But first he had a public lesson to get across.

Which may be why one of the cowboys, seeing his champion about to lose, lost his head. By now the crowd had formed a semicircle around the two combatants. Raider stiffened as he saw the cowboy slip around behind Earp, then reach for his pistol. Maybe he intended to shoot Earp in the back, or maybe he only meant to throw down on him.

Raider never found out. Masterson, who'd been standing behind Earp all the time, holding Earp's holstered pistol in his left hand, with the belt trailing down, simply pointed the end of the holster at the cowboy. Wrapping his right hand around the pistol's butt, he cocked the hammer. "Bang—you're dead," Masterson murmured to the cowboy, his voice as cold as ice.

The cowboy froze. But he was not alone in his unsportsman-like behavior. Another cowboy had slipped halfway around behind Masterson, and was clawing for his holstered pistol. Unfortunately for him, he was standing only a couple of feet away from Raider, who casually twisted the pistol from the cowboy's grip the moment it left the holster. Raising the pistol so that the muzzle was against the cowboy's temple, Raider cocked the hammer. "Let's say we just watch the fight, pil-grim," Raider said, smiling at the startled young man.

There was not much more fight to watch. Hiram could no longer hold up his hands. Earp hit him in the stomach one more time, then clubbed a savage, chopping right downward against the point of his jaw. Hiram went down like a poleaxed steer. A puff of dust rose when his massive body hit the ground. He made a slight swimming motion, as if to get up, then he collapsed again, unmoving.

A collective groan passed among the cowhands. Two of them tried to get Hiram back on his feet, but it was clear that he was finished. Earp turned to retrieve his revolver from Mas-terson. His gaze flicked to the man Masterson was covering, then almost immediately to Raider, who still had the cowboy's pistol pressed against his temple. "You keep coming up with guns,'' Earp said dryly, as he took his gunbelt from Masterson and buckled it on.

"Guns like me," Raider replied, deadpan.

Earp looked back at him, equally unsmiling, then he turned back toward the cowboys. "Pistols, boys," he snapped. "Pile 'em up on the boardwalk."

The cowhands, sullen because of the beating Earp had given their champion, milled about angrily for a moment, but by now Earp and Bat Masterson were no longer alone. Ed Masterson, Bat's brother, also an assistant marshal, had come on the scene, carrying a nasty-looking, ten-gauge, sawed-off, double-barreled shotgun, which was pointed in the cowboys' general direction. Within minutes there was a considerable pile of hardware decorating the boardwalk, from old pre-war cap and ball revolvers, to a single-shot Barnes boot pistol. "You get 'em back when you leave town, boys," Earp told the cowhands, most of whom were looking a little sheepish by now. The crowd began to break up, individual men drifting off to their particular end-of-trail vices.

Earp and Ed Masterson scooped up the guns and began carting them into the marshal's office. Bat walked over to Raider. "Thanks for backing me up," Masterson said, sticking out a hand.

Raider took the other man's hand, returning a firm handshake. Standing so close, he had a good chance to more fully appraise Masterson. He was a much different man than Earp, who was best known for his huge walrus mustaches and cold eyes. Masterson was about ten years younger than Earp, in his early twenties, smaller, and a dandy, complete with well-fitting suit, vest, watch chain, stickpin for his tie, and a neatly-brushed derby, set at a rakish angle on his neatly-barbered head. His eyes were of an amazingly light, soft blue. Friendly eyes, set off by a soft, full moustache. A friendly-looking man, but not a weak one.

Raider nodded. "I don't like back-shootin'."

Masterson appraised him openly. "Say," he finally said. "You ever thought about becoming a lawman?"

CHAPTER FIVE

Raider's intrusion into Wyatt Earp's fight with the cowboy champion had an unexpected result: a new friendship for Raider. Not with Earp, who still treated him aloofly, but with Bat Masterson.

The friendship was very useful to Raider; he now found himself in the middle of Dodge City life, among the movers and shakers, privy to the mass of gossip, rumor, and plain fantasy that swirled through the town's saloons, whorehouses, and restaurants.

Then there was the friendship itself. Raider liked Bat. Half the town seemed to like him. The other half hated him, partly because of his connection to the political element that wanted the town to stay wide-open and woolly. Raider found Bat to be inquisitive, friendly, sunny, and full of information.

One evening Raider and Bat left Delmonico's Restaurant, on their way to a card game at the Long Branch. They were passing behind a large freight wagon when Raider saw Benjamin Hill, and his coterie of Latins, walking by a lighted window. Raider stopped, and stood watching Hill. Bat stopped beside him. Bat said nothing until Hill had passed, and Raider had started on his way again. "I've seen you watching Hill before," Bat said, catching up to Raider. "Does it have anything to do with that man you shot?"

"Rafe? He was Hill's man."

Bat nodded. "I always thought so. A moron like Rafe never would have been able to keep hold of that saloon on his own."

Raider glanced over at Bat. "Sounds like you're interested in Hill, too."

Bat let a few seconds pass before answering. "There's— just something about Hill that doesn't quite add up. Oh, he seldom gets into real trouble, but it gives me the creeps the way Hill and those three little weasels drift around together. It's a feeling like, well, like turning over a rock and finding a bunch of scorpions piled on top of each other."

"Who are they, those men with Hill?" Raider asked.

Bat shrugged. "Don't really know. Wyatt told me they aren't Mexicans. Wrong accent. But Hill talks to them in Spanish all the time; I don't know if any of the three speak English at all."

"But you're interested in 'em."

More silence, then Bat said, "A woman got her throat cut about a month back. I think it was one of those three men. Or maybe all three. It wasn't just her throat; somebody raped her, beat her up pretty bad, then cut the shit outta her. I'd seen one of Hill's men watching her the day before. She was a whore, and I heard some complaints that she wasn't above separating a customer from his wallet, but she sure as hell didn't deserve that kind of treatment."

"How 'bout Hill hisself?" Raider asked. "Could he have been in on it?"

"Could be. But maybe I'm barking up the wrong tree. Maybe that woman fleeced some old buffalo hunter, and he used his skinning knife to pay her back."

They were on the boardwalk now, in front of Varieties, the town's finest dance hall and gambling palace. Bat stopped at the doorway and waved to the bartender, another of his brothers, George. George waved back. He had the same light blue eyes as Bat. Bat was about to move on, but he stopped again, tapped Raider on the arm, and jerked his chin toward the rear of the room. "See that woman back there?" he asked. "The one talking to the dance hall girls?"

Raider scanned the room, then saw a dark-haired woman standing facing four young dime-a-dance girls. From the way the girls were hanging their heads, she must be chewing them out. The woman was partly facing away from Raider, but even so, he had an impression of a handsome woman, very well constructed. "Yeah, I see her," he said to Bat.

"She could tell you a lot about Hill," Bat replied. "She used to be his woman."

Bat turned and began to walk along the boardwalk again. "Come on," he called to Raider. "Let's head on over to the Long Branch before we get squeezed out of the game."

Raider hung back for a moment, looking at the woman. She must have sensed he was there, because she turned and looked straight at him. For two or three seconds Raider and the woman looked directly at one another. He noticed that her gaze did not waver. And then Bat was calling for him again. Raider took one more look at the woman, then turned and hurried down the boardwalk after Bat.

Raider learned that the woman's name was Nanna. He said nothing more about her to Bat that night; the game, a fierce game of seven card stud, required his total concentration. The next morning, however, he and Bat were sitting in chairs on the front veranda of the Dodge House, hoping that a little fresh air would clear away their hangovers. Casually, bit by bit, as if only to pass the time, Raider extracted Nanna's history from Bat, as much of it as Bat knew, which was little enough.

"She's not the average dance hall girl," Bat told Raider. "I don't think she's a prostitute, either. Oh, she skates around the fringes of being a whore, but never quite seems to fall over the edge. Seems to have some education, a good upbringing. A real smart woman. I wonder what the hell she's doing here?"

"What the hell are we doin' here?" Raider muttered morosely.

"Why," Bat exclaimed, with the exuberance of his youth, "having one hell of a good time!"

Now that he was on the subject of Nanna, Bat seemed unable

to leave it. Which suited Raider. He wondered if Bat might not be just a little bit sweet on her.

"She sure as hell isn't any shrinking violet, not one of those innocent young things," Bat continued. "She's had her men, but she's picky about it. Chooses her own, doesn't let them choose her."

"Then how the hell," Raider asked incredulously, "did she get tangled up with a man like Hill?"

"Now, that's a good question. But I don't have any good answers. Nanna's a real moody woman. She was real down just before she got hooked up with Hill. Seemed like she just kind of cracked open for a while."

"How long did it last? Her and Hill, I mean."

Bat thought a moment. "About three months. But I think it got kind of difficult after the first month. Hill started acting like he owned her. Just before the end, Nanna showed up a couple of times with black eyes. I'd guess that Mister Hill doesn't mind hitting women."

"And she put up with that?" Raider remembered that one long moment when his and Nanna's eyes had met. He had gotten an impression of force, of strength. It had not been the look of a woman weak enough to put up with abuse from a man.

Bat grinned. "Not for long. She just kinda stopped seeing him. You could tell he didn't like that; he'd glare at her whenever they passed in the street. One night he walked right into Varieties, grabbed her by the arm, and told her she was coming with him. Used some really dirty language. Well, Nanna reached right in between her tits and pulled out this little over-under deringer. Stuck it right between Hill's eyes and told him that if he didn't let go of her, she'd kill him on the spot. Didn't really raise her voice much, but oh, it was a cold voice. I really think she was just about to pull the trigger.

"Well, Hill let go of her like he'd just burnt his hand. Then she told him that if he ever bothered her again, she'd kill him one way or another, even if it was in his sleep. Hill didn't like that, but there were a lot of people around, lots of her friends, so he just turned around and beat it out of there. I haven't seen him near her since. But I've seen him look at her from across the street. If he could, he'd kill her.''

Raider was thoughtfully sucking on a toothpick. "Sounds like quite a woman.''

Bat grinned. "You sound interested.''

Now Raider grinned. "Well, a man has t' have somethin' in life b'sides whiskey an' cards.''

He made it sound like a simple case of light, uncomplicated lust. But he had already realized that Nanna might be a key to what he was looking for: information on Hill. It was an old Agency practice to try to get close to people who were close to your target, even old Allan Pinkerton's strict Scotch morality wavered badly whenever sin had a chance of producing practical results.

Raider began spending time in Varieties, ostensibly to gamble, but also to be close to Nanna. She was in charge of the dance hall girls. She protected them from over-eager men, and disciplined them when they got out of line. Raider never saw Nanna herself dance with a man.

She knew he was there, and she seemed to sense that he was there for her. Perhaps it had been that one long look they'd interchanged the first time he'd seen her. Perhaps it was something in his manner now. At times he had trouble taking his eyes off her. She was quite beautiful, with long, lustrous, dark brown hair, and a lovely face dominated by large, dark eyes. There seemed to be nothing artificial about the way she filled out her dress.

But it was her manner, even more than her beauty, that fascinated Raider. Her movements were a blend of grace and strength. Bat had gotten it right; Nanna made no attempt to mimic the shy, simpering little virgin, as some of her dance hall girls did. She exuded—what? Independence?

Yes, independence. But underlying her independence, her beauty, there was something else. Something dark and brooding. A core of unhappiness, only half-hidden.

They had not yet spoken to one another; yet more and more frequently, their eyes met. Raider wondered why he did not just walk up to Nanna and start a conversation. Other men talked to her, and she would often reply animatedly. Something was causing him to hesitate, as if his first words to her would be an occasion too important to chance handling poorly.

Important? Yes, he could feel it. He tried to tell himself that this was because she might help him nail Hill. But he knew, sensed somewhere inside himself, that this feeling of importance, of something pending, had other roots. And it scared him a little. If a man wanted to remain free, he chose women for whom he felt as little as possible.

One night Raider was in Varieties, playing a game of cards with some cattle buyers from Saint Louis. The table at which he was playing was close to the dance floor. Nanna was seated at a table only a few feet away, keeping an eye on her girls. Raider glanced at her, studying her face, which seemed especially brooding tonight. And beautiful.

Then he saw her look up, scanning her girls, her eyes suddenly wary. Yes, there was trouble coming; not from a cowboy, but from a slicker of some kind, a man dressed in a checked suit, wearing fancy kidskin shoes. He was grinning, while he tugged one of the girls closer to him than she apparently wanted to be. Raider saw the man's hands pawing at the bodice of the girl's low-cut dress; he was trying to slide his fingers down inside, to fondle her breasts. The girl had seized the man's roving hand, but he was obviously too strong for her. Still grinning, he finally managed to work his hand down between the girl's rather large breasts.

Nanna rose smoothly from her chair, and in two long strides, was standing next to the man. "Take your hands off that girl," she said icily.

The man left his hand where it was. "Well, well," he said loudly, still grinning, "whatta we got here? Little Miss Icy-Ass."

He seemed to know Nanna. She met his stare. "I said, take your dirty hands off her."

He scowled. "Look, bitch. I paid for this dance, an' I'm gonna dance it the way I see fit."

He must have pinched the girl's breast, because she yelled. Nanna reached up, took hold of the man's thumb, and twisted hard. Now it was the man's turn to yell. He jerked his hand away from the girl's breast, but now his eyes were hot, angry.

"Fuckin' bitch!" he shouted, abruptly shoving Nanna hard in the chest, sending her reeling backward.

The man was actually in big trouble now. Molesting women in public was definitely a violation of the local code of conduct. You might get away with gunning other men down, you might cut a man's face to ribbons with a broken whiskey bottle, you might even beat a woman up, as long as you did it privately. But to publicly lay hands on a woman, especially a woman as well-known as Nanna, was an invitation to a bullet in the gut. Any one of a dozen men in the saloon might have proceeded to extract atonement from the man in the loud checked suit, but Raider was closest, and he moved the fastest. Walking straight up to the man, he backhanded him across the face as hard as he could.

The man reeled backward, his back hitting the bar. "What the—?" he howled, his hand going to his face, which was now marred by an angry red blotch. A slow trickle of blood was leaking from his lower lip.

Raider walked up to him again. The man flinched, perhaps expecting another backhand to the face, which Raider was not about to give him, because the back of his hand hurt like hell. He knew better than to backhand a man; too much tender, unpadded bone. He could have broken his Goddamn right hand. His gun hand.

For a moment Raider and the man in the checked suit stood glaring at one another. However, within a very short time, the man in the suit had read a lot of disquieting things in those cold black eyes staring so hard into his own. Perhaps his death. He lowered his gaze, shrinking back against the bar. "No offense," he muttered.

By now Nanna had come up. She had a dime in her hand. She flipped it at the man in the checked suit. It hit his chest and bounced off, rolling onto the dirty floor. "There's your money, big spender," she snarled. "Now, get the hell out of here."

The man made no move for the dime, but remained standing against the bar, his eyes hunting out everything but Raider or Nanna. Raider, snorting in disgust, turned away and started back toward his table. He had to pass right by Nanna; their arms would brush. He looked into her eyes, which were flicking from him to the man at the bar. She was obviously very angry. He would have liked to have been there when she pulled that deringer on Hill.

Then, a sudden widening of her eyes alerted him. "Look out!" she started to shout, but Raider was already turning.

The man in the checked suit, the man whom both Raider and Nanna had humiliated, had seized an empty whisky bottle by the neck, and was swinging it downward, as hard as he could, aiming at Raider's head. Raider looked straight into the twisted snarl of hatred, rage, and cowardice distorting the man's features, then he simply stepped to the man's right, very close to him, so that he and the man were almost facing in the same direction, and as the bottle descended in a wild arc, he let his hand follow the other man's hand. It was very easy to gently take hold of the bottle, near the neck, and twist it from the man's grip.

The man in the suit staggered forward, thrown off balance. For a second he stared in amazement, first at his empty hand, then at the bottle, which was now in Raider's hand. It was a short, horrified look, then he blurted out, "Oh, God!" and turned and ran for the door.

Raider idly tossed the bottle into the air, caught it, then set it on the bar. When he turned, he saw Nanna looking at him, with a knowing little half-smile on her lips. He suddenly felt like a school kid showing off for the girl down the street. "Thanks for the warning," he muttered.

Nanna laughed outright. "Warning? You didn't need any warning. When you turned your back on that man, you were setting him up."

Raider grinned sheepishly. It was true. He'd been fairly certain that the man's damaged pride would demand some kind of satisfaction. He'd seen the bottle sitting so conveniently close to the man's hand. He'd used Nanna's eyes as his warning device. When they'd widened, he'd moved.

Still laughing, Nanna invited him to sit with her. They exchanged banalities, neither of them talking about much of anything, as if they were fencing, probing, testing. Raider could sense the woman's interest in him; he could tell by the way her eyes would occasionally examine him, rove for just a second or two over his body, then move back up to study his face.

But it was not going to be that easy. After an hour, Nanna excused herself. "I'm not paying enough attention to the girls," she said. But Raider knew it was not the girls. Nanna could see them well enough from where they were sitting. It was as if a veil had suddenly descended over her eyes, dimming the life, the interest, that had been shining within them just a moment before.

Raider had the sense to utter a few more pleasantries, then leave. But he came back the next night, and the next. Each night went much like the first; an hour or two of lively, witty animation from Nanna, then that descending veil. By the fourth night, he was just about ready to give the whole thing up. Then she surprised him. They'd been laughing about something a humorous drunk had said, when suddenly the veil descended again. But this time Nanna did not take her eyes from his. She looked straight at him, studying his face, as if she expected to be enlightened. "What is it you want?" she asked abruptly. Then she got up and walked quickly toward a door near the rear of the room.

Raider remained seated. Yeah, he asked himself. What the hell do I want? Hill? The end of this assignment? Or Nanna?

The next night, he debated whether or not to go back to Varieties. Hell, you son of a bitch, why not just leave her alone?

He convinced himself that he'd go because of the booze. Most of the saloons in Dodge served various brands of diluted snake venom under the name of whiskey, but at Varieties, George Masterson was ready to provide the discerning drinker with much finer potations. Over the past few days, with Nanna's urging, Raider had been sampling some fine French brandy. He was developing a taste for the brandy that was at serious odds with his budget.

Nanna was at her usual table. She looked solemnly at Raider as he approached. He stood near her chair, hesitating. "Aren't you going to sit down?" she finally asked. "I'll send one of the girls over to get you a brandy."

He sat. Neither he nor Nanna had much to say, just desultory little batches of words. Raider's drink came. He began drinking it too quickly to savor the fine taste. He was uneasy. Something about tonight was different. Nanna seemed so—preoccupied. Was she losing interest in their nightly conversations? That light, bantering tone was gone from her voice.

Finally, she looked up. Her eyes were big dark pools, only inches from his own. "Do you know where I live?" she asked abruptly.

Surprised, he merely nodded. She had a room, or rooms, upstairs, at the back of the building.

"Meet me there in half an hour. Come up the back stairs."

She stood up abruptly, then left the room, going out by the door near the back. Raider stared after her, until he realized his mouth was hanging open. He sucked hard at his brandy, draining the glass; then he got up and went over to the bar and ordered another from George. "What got into Nanna?" George asked casually.

Raider shook his head. "I dunno."

"Moody," George replied. "A moody woman."

The next half hour limped by on badly crippled feet. Finally, it was time. "Well, see you 'round," Raider muttered to George, putting his third glass down on the bar.

George looked at him inscrutably. "Yeah."

Raider wandered out onto the street. It was the usual mad scene; drunken cowboys staggering by, singing, cursing, or vomiting. Light spilled from the open doorways of saloons, gambling halls, and whorehouses. Dodge City on an average night.

Raider walked around the block, into the alley that ran behind Front Street. It was as dark as sin; he instantly wondered if he'd been set up. God, he wished he had a gun!

It took a little doing, in the dark, to find the stairs Nanna had mentioned. He started up them, swearing as they creaked loudly under his weight.

There was a door at the top. Dim light filtered through a gap at the bottom. He raised his hand to knock, then stopped himself. She'd said to meet her here. He'd been invited.

Raider tried the knob. The door was not locked. He opened it and stepped inside. His eyes scanned the room, then came to rest on a fascinating sight. Nanna was lying on a bed, only a few feet away. Naked. In the dim light of an oil lamp that had been turned down low, her flesh gleamed golden. My God, he wondered. How could her clothes have hidden all that?

Her hands were behind her head, which pulled her breasts upward, high and taut. They were big, full, firm-looking breasts. She was looking at him calmly. "A half hour can seem like a long time, can't it?" she murmured.

He noticed that her voice was now pitched lower than normal, there was a peculiar huskiness to it. He sensed the huskiness in his own voice. "Too damned long," he growled, heading for the bed.

CHAPTER SIX

Raider lay in bed, staring up at the sagging, splintery boards that formed the ceiling. Nanna had made attempts to soften the roughness of her rooms—a little lace, some flowers, a few pictures on the walls—but it sure as hell wasn't the Ritz.

She lay beside him, asleep. His hand was on her breast. He felt her breathing pick up, become rushed, anxious. He looked over at her, saw her face contort. She was dreaming again. Dreaming about whatever private hell lived inside her head.

He lightly squeezed the breast on which his hand lay. It was resilient, solid, beautifully formed. He felt the nipple stiffen against his palm, but she did not awaken.

It had been a hot night; the blankets were pulled down a little past her waist. He studied her body, the richness of it, the large breasts, her surprisingly slender waist, the outswell of hips where they disappeared beneath the sheet. A few inches below her navel, he could see the beginning of a soft tangle of curly brown hair.

He looked up at her face. A few minutes ago it had been peaceful, relaxed in sleep. Now, unknown emotions were chas-

41

ing each other across her features as the dreaming continued. He wondered what the dream was about. She'd never told him what any of her dreams were about. She would wake up in a cold sweat, terror in her eyes, until she realized where she was, that she was safe. And say nothing.

Two weeks. It had been two weeks since he'd first made his way up the stairs to her rooms. Two weeks in which he should have been using her to stalk Hill. But he hadn't done it, not because of any scruples, but because of his fascination with Nanna herself, the contradictions of her, the joy and the despair. She had claimed all of his attention.

He couldn't figure her out. Every time he thought he had the key, some new facet of her character would surface. It was as if there was a whole lot of Nannas inside her beautiful body.

The first time he'd seen her in one of her depressions, he'd been alarmed, wondering if someone had done something to her, had hurt or insulted her. She'd been sitting in the chair by her dresser, staring into a corner, her face blank. Tears were running slowly, soundlessly down her cheeks. Yet, within ten minutes she'd been straddling his body, naked, engulfing him, her face alight with wild triumph, her hips churning against his own, her long dark hair flying around her shoulders as she raced from one orgasm to another.

She usually did not drink, but he had seen her drunk twice, both times in her room, terribly drunk, cursing under her breath, muttering incomprehensible things. He'd thought it might be about her family, but she never talked about her family, never even suggested that she had one.

Her lovemaking was as many-faceted as Nanna herself. Sometimes she would make love to him for hours, slowly, languorously, as if they had all the time in the world. Her soft, warm flesh would slide against his own. Her eyes would fill with a distant, deep passion.

Then there were other images. Of Nanna screaming, moaning, thrashing, begging for more. "Harder! Faster!" she would cry out. Her face would twist into a mask of wild orgiastic passion, full of half-hidden desperation, as if the act of making love would somehow save her from—what?

Raider knew that he'd caught a tiger, literally, by the tail.

And what a tail. He knew he should just walk away from her, but he also knew that he could not do that. It wasn't just their lovemaking that held him, her beauty and passion, but something in her that drew him like a magnet. Perhaps a shadow of dark reflections inside his own soul.

He made no mention of Hill. He did not want to talk about Hill, to think of him using her body. So he let his original reason for pursuing Nanna languish. Until Hill himself broke the stalemate.

One day Raider and Nanna were walking along Front Street's boardwalk. He liked to be seen with her, and she seemed proud of him, almost as if she were showing him off. They were walking arm in arm. This was one of Nanna's bright, alive days. She had turned to Raider, was saying something about Bat Masterson, when they almost ran head-on into Benjamin Hill.

He and his three Latins had just stepped out of a saloon, onto the boardwalk. Hill stopped, abruptly, directly in front of Raider and Nanna. His eyes shifted back and forth between them. Raider read shock, anger, hatred in those cold gray eyes. From their savage glitter, he half-expected Hill to assault him, perhaps to order his men to gun him down.

Then Hill abruptly pushed past, his men following. Raider watched him go, just in case Hill turned, pulled a gun, started firing. But Hill continued on down the street.

Raider turned toward Nanna. She was looking after Hill, too. He tried to read her expression. Hatred? Fear? Perhaps a little of both.

She said nothing, and in a moment was chatting away as gaily as before, although Raider thought he could detect an edge of worry behind her surface cheerfulness. He decided to play her game, say nothing. If she wanted to pretend that Hill had never existed, he would go along.

Hill, however, had other ideas. Raider was leaving Delmonico's one night, leisurely picking his teeth, when he was suddenly confronted by Hill. Raider looked around quickly; the three Latins were fanned out about twenty yards away, watching him intently. Oh, shit, Raider thought.

Hill stood six feet from Raider, his face twisted with anger.

"You're beginning to intrude way too far into my life, mister," Hill snarled. "If you want to keep breathing, stay away from my woman."

Raider was about to retort that Nanna had not the slightest intention of being Hill's woman, but Hill had already spun around and was walking away, with his men following a few steps behind. Raider shrugged, then headed for Varieties. And Nanna.

However, that night, when they were in bed, after a particularly strenuous bout of lovemaking, Nanna finally brought up the subject of Hill. "Maybe you should go away," she said abruptly.

"Huh? You tired o' me?"

She turned toward him. Her features were still flushed, her body damp from exertion. "Never," she insisted. "But one of my girls was out on the street today. She heard what Hill said to you. He's a dangerous man. If he said he'd kill you, he will."

Raider looked at her coolly. "Better men than him have tried. They ain't no longer around."

She shook her head in exasperation. "You don't understand. He won't meet you face to face. He'll arrange something cowardly, a back-shooting."

"I'll watch my back."

She hesitated. "Then I can't talk you into going away?"

He slowly shook his head. "Only if we get tired of each other."

She smiled a little. He could tell she was glad. But she was still worried. She began to talk about Hill, sometimes a little distractedly. "He's the coldest man I've ever known," she said. She laughed bitterly. "And I've known a lot of men—in that well-known Biblical way."

She seemed to anticipate his next question. "Why did I ever get involved with a snake like Ben Hill? All that I can figure is that I must have been trying to punish myself. God knows I need punishment. Well, he was a willing instrument."

Her voice grew hard. "He's one cruel son of a bitch!"

She suddenly dropped the subject. "What about you?" She asked. "Why are you here in Dodge? You just drift around, play cards, drink, fuck dance-hall women. Somehow, that picture, an aimless drifter, doesn't seem to fit you.''

He shrugged. ''Mebbe I need punishin', too,'' he replied lightly. But he did not feel light inside. If she ever learned that he was a Pinkerton, that he was here to trap the man who'd been her lover, that he'd originally planned to use her to find out more about Hill—

Damn, but she made him feel uneasy! Every instinct had warned him about getting tied up too tightly with a woman. But damned if he could control himself when he was around Nanna.

He was still mulling over his situation the next evening, walking along the street, kicking at the drier piles of horse droppings. His mind was full of Hill, wondering what the bastard might have done to Nanna when they were together, hating the man whenever he thought of Hill touching her body, especially hating Hill when he imagined Nanna responding. Having first-hand knowledge of Nanna's passion, of the depth of it, he could not imagine her not responding. And the son of a bitch had hurt her.

He suddenly stopped. He was directly in front of one of the seedier bars. He could see in through the open doorway. Hill was standing at the bar, talking to a man. Raider recognized the other man. Bat had pointed him out just the day before. ''Gunman up from Texas,'' Bat had told him. ''Mean as a snake. Kills for fun. There's a story that he shot a woman and her kids over in New Mexico, did it just out of meanness. I think we oughta run him out of town. Hell, we oughta run half the people in Dodge out of town.''

Hill and the gunman—what the hell was his name?—Rawls. That was it. Dirty Jack Rawls. The two men were deep in conversation. Now why would a man in Hill's position, a man who'd gone out of his way to keep his skirts clean, be buddying up to an animal like Rawls?

Raider put it out of his mind, but later that night, after a rather uninteresting poker game at the Long Branch, Bat asked Raider to walk over to the marshal's office with him. Once inside, they sat down on rickety chairs. ''There's a rumor goin' around town,'' Bat said, ''that Ben Hill has it in for you.''

Raider smiled. "Funny. Hill told me the same thing hisself."

Bat shook his head angrily. "It's no joke, Raider. The man's a belly-crawling reptile. If he wants you dead, he'll do his best to see that you end up full of holes. Or with your throat cut."

Raider cocked his head to one side. "Are you suggestin' I leave town? Go runnin' off with my tail 'tween my legs?"

Bat smiled. "I don't insult my friends. I've got a better idea."

He walked over to an old battered desk, pulled open a drawer, and took out a gun and holster. Raider saw that it was the Sheriff's Special Colt forty-five that Wyatt Earp had confiscated from him after he'd shot Rafe.

Bat unwound a bunch of straps. "It's a shoulder rig that belonged to that Mississippi gambler who got himself killed last week," Bat said. "Fits your Colt pretty damned good. Here, try it on."

Raider picked up the contraption, then set about finding the correct way to attach the various straps and buckles around his body. When it was in place, he slipped the short-barreled Colt into the holster. It lay with the butt pointed slightly downward, so that it could be easily pulled from beneath a coat. A spring clip held the pistol firmly in place. "Kinda uncomfortable," Raider said, a big question written all over his face.

"Go ahead. Wear it," Bat insisted. "Wyatt knows I'm doing this. He hates Hill worse'n sin. He'd hate to see him get you or anyone else, just 'cause you couldn't protect yourself."

Raider smiled. "I'll make sure it don't happen. I'd hate t' see Wyatt disappointed."

Nanna noticed the gun that night. "It's because of Hill, isn't it?" she asked.

"Yeah," he replied flatly. She looked at him intently, but did not ask any more questions. That night her lovemaking was especially intense, desperate, seeking. When he left her a few hours before dawn, she was in the middle of one of her dreams. He was tempted to stay with her, comfort her when she awakened. But he had things to do.

He went back to his room for a few hours of sleep. He woke up a little before noon. He was hungry, but he fought off his hunger and set to work on the short-barreled Colt. It was a brand-new pistol; the action was rougher than a dried corncob. If Hill was going to start sending gunmen after him, Raider had better do something about sweetening that action a little, make it function more smoothly.

Digging through his saddlebags, Raider took out a small file. He then disassembled the pistol, and began honing the metal where the trigger sear and the hammer made contact. When he had it the way he wanted it, he reassembled the pistol. Now the trigger pull was sweet and light.

He worked on the hammer spring next, thinning it with the file until it was much easier to cock the pistol. Dry-firing several times, he noticed that the action was slightly out of time; the cylinder latch did not engage early enough. During fast firing, the holes in the cylinder might not line up correctly with the barrel. It took another half hour to file the cylinder lock and pawl until they were just the right lengths.

He hesitated before beginning the next alteration. Finally he decided to go ahead. He'd never do anything like this to his full-sized pistol, one of the new Colt Peacemakers, with a seven-inch barrel. It lay at the bottom of his saddlebags, as Wyatt Earp's rules required. But the little Sheriff's Special was basically a belly gun, for close-range killing, face to face. The most important thing would be to get the damned thing out fast, and into action.

So he cut away the front of the trigger guard, leaving just enough to protect the back of the trigger. Now his finger would slide into place against the trigger the moment he gripped the butt. Finally, he filed away most of the front sight, so that there would be nothing to catch against his coat when he reached for the gun.

When he left his room late that afternoon, half-starved, Raider was wearing the altered pistol under his left shoulder, in the shoulder rig Bat had given him. It took a little getting used to; he kept wanting to shrug his shoulder, but he knew that he must not. He would give away the position of the pistol.

After a meal at Delmonico's—he'd been winning enough at poker lately to afford the place—he ambled over to Varieties. George was behind the bar as usual, and Nanna was keeping an eagle eye on her girls, toward the back of the room. Raider leaned against the bar, smiled at Nanna, and ordered a beer. George was still drawing the beer when Raider heard the swinging doors bang open behind him. He turned his head. Dirty Jack Rawls was standing in the doorway, grinning straight at Raider.

Raider saw that Rawls was wearing a gun belt. A Remington Beals cap and ball pistol, the thirty-six caliber Navy model, filled the holster. The pistol's butt had a worn, well-used look. Raider wondered if it had any notches. The ape grinning at him from the doorway looked like the kind of man who'd cut notches in his gun butt.

Rawls was a medium-tall, beefy man. There was nothing elegant about him at all. His broad, flat face was fuzzed by a three-day growth of reddish beard. His eyes glared with ignorance and meanness. Jack Rawls was obviously the kind of man whose passing would leave the world a much better place.

"Well, what the hell we got us here?" Rawls said in a loud braying voice, as he walked around Raider and took a place at the bar farther inside the room. Looking past Rawls, Raider saw Nanna suddenly look up.

Rawls leaned against the bar nonchalantly, left side to the bar, with his gun hand unimpeded. Raider could see that he'd had experience. "Your name Raider?" Rawls asked bluntly.

"So they say," Raider replied casually.

Rawls stared at him for another few seconds. "I've come here to kill you," he said, just as bluntly as before.

"Hey!" George Masterson cut in from behind the bar. "You can't talk like that in here. And you're supposed to check your gun. You can have it back when you leave."

Rawls slowly turned his head and looked straight at George. "Shut your fuckin' mouth, barkeep, or I'll kill you next."

No, Raider reflected, Hill had not hired the smoothest mannered gunman around, but he sure got right down to business, no fooling around at all. Rawls obviously figured Raider wasn't armed, so he probably just planned on gunning him down, then getting out of town with whatever money Hill had given him. Simple, fast, and effective.

Farther back in the saloon, behind Rawls, Nanna had finally understood what was happening. She quickly began to shepherd her girls out of the way. Good, Raider thought. One less thing to worry about.

However, the room was not yet quite clear of innocent by-standers, and Raider had a definite impression that Rawls was about to start shooting. Maybe he'd better stall things a little. "Are you Dirty Jack Rawls?" Raider asked abruptly.

As he'd expected, Rawls was in love with the sound of his own name. "Yeah," he replied, grinning. "Guess you've maybe heard of me, huh?"

Raider smiled back at him. "Sure have. Heard that you murdered some women and kids down in New Mexico. I also heard that you're a cowardly, back-shootin', gutless belly-crawler. Mebbe it's time somebody killed you, Rawls."

It was slowly dawning on Rawls that the man he was facing did not appear to be afraid of him at all, even though he'd just promised to kill him. Which led Rawls to the conclusion that maybe Raider wasn't unarmed at all. But he also figured, correctly, that if the man facing him had a hideout gun, it would take him longer to get to it than it would take Rawls to draw his Remington, the butt of which lay only inches from his right hand.

Raider could tell when Rawls was ready to start his draw. He saw it first in his eyes, then in the tensing of his muscles. Raider made no immediate move for his gun. A heavy shot glass lay only inches from his right hand. He scooped it up and threw it straight at Rawls.

The heavy little glass caught Rawls on the cheekbone, disorienting him for a split second, just long enough for Raider to reach inside his coat for his Sheriff's Special. His finger slid past the missing trigger guard and onto the trigger itself, just the way he'd planned. He was standing less than six feet from Rawls. He merely pointed the muzzle of his little forty-five straight at Rawls's chest, then, holding the trigger back, Raider fanned the hammer three times with his left hand, so quickly that it was difficult to distinguish the sound of the separate shots.

It was not the best shooting Raider had ever done, but every bullet slammed, in a six-inch-wide pattern, right into the center of Rawls's chest.

Rawls staggered backward, his still uncocked pistol spinning from his hand. He hit the floor hard; Raider could see his head bounce against the planks. Raider stood over him, with the Sheriff's Special cocked again, pointed at Rawls's face. But there was no need to fire. Rawls stared past Raider, up at the ceiling, as if he had just seen the most amazing sight. Then, a second later, Dirty Jack Rawls, killer, back-shooter, hired gun, breathed his last.

CHAPTER SEVEN

Nanna lay panting beside Raider. He ran his hand over her sweat-slick belly, while he did a little panting himself. Damn, he thought ruefully, she's more likely to kill me than Rawls ever was.

He'd seen it before, passion induced by the nearness of death. Once Rawls's body had been carted off to the undertaker, and the formalities taken care of, with George Masterson swearing to his brother and Wyatt Earp that it was a clear case of self-defense, Raider and Nanna had headed straight for her rooms, where they had pulled off their clothes and proceeded to try to fuck one another to death.

Raider looked over at Nanna. Her face was still flushed from the violence of her last orgasm, but her expression was hardly radiant. "He won't stop just because you killed his hired gun," she said abruptly. "He'll try again. He'll keep trying until you're dead."

"Or he is. Or till I've found 'nough evidence t' put 'im where he cain't—"

Raider quickly shut his mouth, but Nanna sensed his sudden tension. "Evidence?" she asked. "What are you talking about?"

She levered herself up onto an elbow and looked him straight in the face. Her left breast was pressing against his right arm; he was very aware of it. "Tell me, Raider," she insisted. "Tell me the truth. Ever since I first met you I've known you aren't what you say you are. Just—tell me."

Raider looked into her beautiful face. He could not lie any more. "I'm a Pinkerton," he said. "I was sent here t' nail Hill."

Nanna froze. They were each propped up on one arm, looking into one another's face, bodies tense. "And you knew I used to be his—woman," Nanna finally said, almost under her breath. "You wanted to—"

"At first. But once I got t' know you, I couldn't just—use you."

She didn't seem to have heard him. "A Pinkerton," she murmured. "I'm in bed with a Pinkerton."

Raider did not know which was bothering her more; the idea he had attempted to use her, or that he was a Pinkerton. The Agency was not at all popular among working people; it was too well known for union-busting, for backing the rich and powerful.

Nanna lay back down. Raider remained on one elbow, studying her face. She was looking up at the ceiling impassively. "I said that I couldn't make myself use you," he repeated.

"I heard you," she said quietly, still looking up at the ceiling. Her face was devoid of emotion. "Maybe I even believe you. But—"

"The hell with Hill," Raider said savagely. "Let's forgit Hill. They can send another man after 'im."

Nanna laughed bitterly. "But that won't stop Hill from coming after you. We're a real pair. We've both wished a lot of trouble on each other."

"Why don't we just git the hell outta this place, leave Hill b'hind us?"

Now she looked at him again, her expression sardonic. "And what would you do? Get a regular job? And maybe I could settle down as sweet little wifey? Don't make a joke out of this, Raider. We are each what we are: a Pink and a bar girl.''

"Don't sell yourself short," Raider started to say heatedly, but Nanna interrupted him. "No lies, Raider. We'll never grow old together, that's just—not reality. So, why don't we take care of our main problem, Benjamin Hill. Later—well, for people like us, later is always a big fat maybe. So, go ahead, tell me exactly why you're here. Surprise me; tell me something about Ben I don't already know."

Raider studied Nanna for several seconds, then realized she was right. So he told her about Hill's suspected involvement in the robberies. Told her a little about his background, what little of it he knew. When he had finished, she slowly shook her head. "The man's more of a snake than I ever imagined," she said softly. Then she smiled, a wry, self-mocking smile. "Boy, can I pick 'em! A back-shooting bandit and a Pinkerton."

The smile was all that kept Raider from getting up and leaving. That, and the fact that he was mother-naked. "Now you tell me 'bout Hill," he said tersely. "Tell me everythin' 'bout him you can remember."

She looked at him oddly for a moment, then began to describe her affair with Hill. He suspected that there was a little cruelty in the way she did it. She spared no details. She described what kind of a lover he was: possessive, driving, cruel. She talked about the things he did to her, and his character, his coldness and greed. And his secretiveness.

"He never did take me to his place," Nanna said. "We always went to a small hotel way out on the edge of town. Plush little place. We always used a suite of rooms, very fancy, with nice furniture. And a big, big bed. That's all I ever saw of that damned hotel, the room and the bed. He'd take me in the back way; the manager would let us in through a private little door back by the alley. It didn't make much sense, because half of the town knew I was sleeping with him. Or maybe it was because of the other men. A lot of stockmen stayed there, men with money. Ben was a jealous bastard. I guessed he was afraid I'd meet some stockman or cattle buyer with more money than he had, and I'd leave him and run off with whoever it was."

Raider had been thinking mostly of Nanna and Hill in that fancy room, on that big bed, but the rest of what she was saying finally began to register. "Huh?" he asked. "What hotel did you say it was?"

"Why, that little place with the stained glass in the front door. Fancy little place. They have Delmonico's send over food for their guests. Treat them really well."

"And the manager used to let Hill in through the back door?" he asked excitedly.

"Yeah," she replied, puzzled by his excitement. "I already told you that. It was almost like Ben owned the place, the way the manager fawned all over him. Nothing but the best for Ben; champagne, room service, and, now that I think of it, they never bothered to give him a bill—unless he paid it when I wasn't around."

Raider was sitting straight up in bed now. "I wouldn't be s'prised if he did own it," he told Nanna. He explained how Hill made a habit of being an invisible backer of various cattle-town businesses. "A perfect setup," Raider mused. "You said that a lot o' stockmen an' cattle buyers stayed there?"

"Yeah. Weren't you listening? Hey—where're you going?"

Raider was feverishly pulling on his clothes. "Gotta send a telegram. Be back in a little while."

Within ten minutes he was at the telegraph office, carefully wording a message to the Agency, asking if any of their "clients" had stayed at the little hotel where Hill and Nanna had had their secret trysts, "clients" being his code for the men who'd been robbed.

The reply did not arrive until late the next morning. It was affirmative; all but one of the robbery victims had stayed at the hotel. Raider took the telegram back up to Nanna's room. She was still in bed, apparently the victim of an overpowering lassitude. Raider tossed the telegram onto the bed. "That's how he does it," he told her triumphantly. "Finds out through the hotel staff who's carryin' money, who's involved in big deals. Mebbe they talk a little too much, let the staff overhear where they're gonna be. Bang. Hill or his men hits 'em."

Nanna looked at him, unsmiling. "Now that you know," she asked, "what are you going to do about it?"

"Set 'im up. Use a decoy. Then, when he comes after the decoy—"

Nanna slowly shook her head. "It won't come out the way you expect. I know. I can feel it."

Raider forced himself to come down from his excitement. He took a closer look at Nanna. Her expression was totally lacking in animation. It bordered on morbidity. "Come on," he urged her. "This way we'll take care 'o Hill, get 'im off our backs. Then—"

"Yes," she replied quietly. "And then."

Raider began to grow annoyed. This was no time to worry about female moods. He laid his hand on her forehead, caressingly, then started for the door. "Where are you going now?" she asked.

"T' see the local law. I cain't do this by myself. I'll need help, cooperation."

Nanna laughed mirthlessly. "Cooperation? From Wyatt Earp? All you'll get from him is used."

"Ah—women!" Raider said disgustedly, then left the room.

Still, it was not Earp that he sought out, but Bat Masterson. Bat began to listen, but halfway through Raider's tale, his mouth fell open. "You?" he burst out. "A Pinkerton?"

"Yeah," Raider said. He took off his hat, smiled, and ran his hands through his hair. "See? No horns. Now listen t' what I'm tellin' you, Goddamn it."

When he'd finished, Bat looked thoughtful. "Hill, huh? So he's the one. I suppose it shouldn't surprise me." He stood up. "Come on. Let's go over and see Wyatt."

They found Earp in the marshal's office, leaning forward in his chair, fanning cards onto a desktop. He looked up, expressionless, as Bat and Raider came in. "Got us something interesting going on," Bat said.

Earp listened quietly while Raider explained why he was in Dodge, but although his face remained without overt expression, Raider thought he could feel excitement building up in the other man. "Hill," Earp finally said, when Raider had finished. "I've always wondered about him and those three little killers who follow him around. Nailing him would be a good day's work."

"Yeah. How are you planning to handle it?" Bat asked Raider.

"Decoy. We can move another Pinkerton operative in here, posing as a stock buyer. He'll move into the hotel an' start talkin' 'bout the big roll he's carryin'. If Hill really is gettin' his information outta that hotel, he'll try for our man. Then we'll take 'im."

"Sounds good," Bat started to say.

"Wait!" Earp cut in. "This isn't Pinkerton work, not here, not in Dodge City. This is our jurisdiction. If Hill is brought down in Dodge, it'll be the local law that does it."

"But how?" Raider burst out. "Hill knows every one o' you. He'd—"

"I know a man we can use as the decoy," Earp replied. "Then we'll nail Hill ourselves. Don't worry, you'll be in on it. But any rewards—"

Raider leaned back in his chair. Rewards. Fame. Earp probably saw himself running for sheriff after he brought in Hill. Or maybe he wanted to be U.S. marshal. And then, of course, there was the reward. A thousand dollars, nearly a year's pay for a town marshal. "Pinkerton operatives cain't accept rewards," Raider said coolly. "It's all yours. Now, where's this man o' yours, this decoy?"

Two days later, when Raider met Earp's man, he nearly called the whole thing off. A damned amateur, Raider thought disgustedly. And, from the bright red of the man's nose, one who drank way too much. Raider pulled Earp aside, out of the man's hearing. "He'll foul it up," he murmured. "He don't look like he has a cool 'nough head t' fool Hill or nobody else."

"Bullshit," Earp snapped. "He's an actor. Stage actor. Real professional. He'll have 'em eating it up like it was caviar."

Oh God, Raider thought. An actor. Once again he thought of calling it off—if he could. No doubt Earp would go through with it on his own. Better to stick close to the operation, try to pull it out of the fire himself in case anything went wrong. Better to try to get the whole thing over with. Then maybe he and Nanna could start things going again. She'd been distant, preoccupied, ever since he'd told her that he was after Hill.

Not that she no longer made love to him; if anything, she made love more fiercely now, as if afraid that each time might be their last.

When he told Nanna about the plan, she slowly shook her head. "Something will go wrong," she said.

"What, for God's sake?" he asked in exasperation.

"Just—something," she insisted. "I can feel it. Inside me."

Raider turned away from her, although he knew that she was right in a way. Lots of things could go wrong. Especially with that clown Earp had called in to play decoy. And as for her feelings, this premonition she kept talking about, well, he'd had too many of his own to completely discount it, but he finally compromised by passing it off as a woman's paranoia.

The actor, his name was Stevens, dutifully checked into the little hotel. He's dressed all wrong, Raider thought, when he saw the man go in through the hotel's front door. He looked more like a drummer than a no-nonsense stock buyer. A loud checked suit, a mohair vest, and shiny shoes with spats. Hell, he looked a little like a pimp.

The plan was fairly simple. Stevens was to let the hotel staff know he was a big eastern cattle buyer, eager to purchase one of the trail herds coming up from Texas. But that was not quite enough. If he simply said he was carrying a lot of money, Hill's men would probably just clout him over the head in some back alley, out of sight, which would make it hard to pin it on Hill, even if they caught one of his men doing it. Instead, Stevens was to casually let the hotel staff get the impression that he intended to pull a fast one, that he was going to ride out onto the prairie all by himself, and meet one of the trail herds a few miles from town, so that he could get first crack at the best cattle.

Just before he left town, he would make a big production of going to the local bank and producing a letter of credit which would allow him to withdraw a large amount of cash. Hill and his men would have no choice, then, other than to hit him out on the open prairie, where Earp, the Masterson brothers, Raider, and another man would be waiting for them.

It took a while to get the plan moving. While Stevens did his part inside the hotel, Earp, Bat, and Raider tried to keep an eye on Hill and his men, and on the hotel staff. Raider knew they just didn't have enough men to do a thorough job. One day, an assistant marshal who'd been watching Hill came into the Long Branch to give Earp his report. Earp, Bat, Luke Short, and Raider were in the middle of a poker game. "Well," Earp asked his man, "what'd Hill do today?"

The assistant marshal shrugged. "Couldn't figure it out. He just stood in the alley behind Front Street and looked up at some stairs and a window. Musta stood there for an hour or more."

"Nanna!" Raider burst out, coming half out of his chair. "I oughta take care of that son of a bitch right now, settle his hash for good."

"Uh-uh!" Earp snapped. "We'll take him the way we planned it. In the meantime, we'll keep a good watch on the girl."

Raider settled back into his seat. He knew why Earp wanted the plan to carry through to the end; he wanted it to look like good police work on his part. And then, on to bigger and better things. That was probably the way the Agency would want it, too. Wrap up the case all nice and neat.

It was fairly easy to discover when Hill was getting ready to make his move. Bat spotted him one day, talking quietly to two hardcases who'd ridden into town the day before—just a couple of days after Hill had sent a telegram to Wichita. "He's usin' outside help," Earp said when he got the news. "But it won't save him this time. Too damned many things linking him to it: the hotel, those two hardcases, and maybe he'll use his own men. Hell, maybe he'll get in on it himself."

The day was chosen. Stevens was to go to the bank about ten in the morning, ostensibly to withdraw ten thousand dollars. Only he would withdraw nothing; when he left the bank, his valise would be stuffed with cut newspaper. Then he would eat lunch at Delmonico's, with the bag clearly visible. After lunch, about one in the afternoon, he would make sure he was seen riding all by himself out onto the prairie. Meanwhile, Raider, the Mastersons, Earp, and a marshal named Bill, would leave town secretly, at eleven, so that they could shadow Stevens, ready to come in on the flank of anyone who attacked him.

But it did not work out quite the way they had planned. Stevens got his newspaper money at ten, all right, but then, sitting in Delmonico's, he began to drink nervously, because he really was nervous; he'd finally figured out that this was not just a play, it was for real; he might end up facing real bandits with real guns. He drank so quickly, and to such devastating effect, that he lost all track of time.

Raider, Earp, and the Mastersons were putting their gear together, ready to ride out in a loop that would put them ahead of Stevens, when one of the town policemen came running into the room. "Goddamn!" the man panted. "Stevens has fucked it up!"

"What? What's happened?" Raider demanded.

"The damned idiot," the policeman wheezed. "He up and left half an hour ago. Just got on his horse, and rode out onto the prairie, drunker'n a skunk. And nobody's seen Hill or his men since early this morning."

CHAPTER EIGHT

After a moment of stunned silence, Raider, Earp, the Masterson brothers, and Bill, the other deputy marshal, broke and ran for their horses, which had not yet been saddled. Raider cursed under his breath as he slung his saddle over his horse's back. He was cursing not at the others, but at himself; this was his fault as much as anyone's. He should have protested more strenuously about the choice of Stevens as a decoy. He should have made this a strictly Pinkerton operation, no matter what Wyatt Earp said. Perhaps his mind had been too full of Nanna and her problems, the threat of Hill hurting her, to think really clearly.

Within ten minutes they were ready to ride, but every one of them realized that they were now at a disadvantage. The plan had been to ride out ahead of Stevens, then ambush Hill and his men. Now they would be playing a game of catch-up. And Stevens had a forty-minute head start.

They rode out of town onto the open range, pushing their horses as hard as they dared. They were slowed by the necessity of keeping on Steven's trail. They did not dare lose him; he could be attacked at any time. Damn! The whole plan had been screwed up by glory-hunting amateurs!

Raider decided to stop swearing at himself and get on with the job. He studied the tracks left by Steven's horse. It was obvious that the actor was pushing the animal way too hard. Maybe he thought that if he went fast, the whole thing would be over with more quickly.

The little posse ended up riding right into the middle of the holdup. Raider heard angry voices ahead, mixed with Stevens's frightened whine. "Goddamn *paper*!" he heard a man shout. It sounded like Hill's voice. "Goddamn worthless paper!" the voice repeated. "It has to be a trap!"

"Come on!" Raider called softly to the other posse members. "Stevens is in big trouble."

Terminal trouble. As the posse topped a rise, they saw Stevens about three hundred yards ahead of them, surrounded by Hill, his three Latins, and the two out-of-town gunmen. Stevens's satchel was lying on the ground, open. Bits of newspaper, cut to the size of currency, were blowing away on the wind. Even as the posse rode into sight, Hill was raising a pistol, aiming it at Stevens. "You tricked me!" they heard Hill scream, the first time Raider had ever seen him lose control so thoroughly.

"No!" Stevens cried out. But it was too late. As Raider started downslope, toward Stevens and his attackers, he saw a puff of white smoke flower from the muzzle of Hill's pistol. He saw Stevens reel in the saddle, both hands pressed to his face in agony. And he heard Stevens's despairing scream as he died.

"Let's get 'em, boys!" he heard Wyatt Earp call out next to him. A moment later the posse was racing toward the bandits, even though they were outnumbered. Even if Earp did not lay the best plans, he sure had guts.

Hill and his men looked up as the posse came thundering down on them. Rifles came up to shoulders. Gunfire crashed. The posse members began firing back. Earp and the Mastersons yipped loudly, standing in their stirrups as they poured fire toward the group of bandits.

Raider saw a bandit go down, one of the men whom Hill

had recently recruited. Bullets were flying all around the posse. We're gonna lose us some men, Raider thought grimly, as he fired his Winchester. It's gonna be one helluva fight.

However, Hill apparently had no desire to stand and shoot it out. He called out something to his Latins, then pulled his horse around and raced toward a pile of boulders that choked off the entrance to a gully. His Latins were right behind him. The remaining bandit hesitated, looked down at his fallen companion for a second, then turned and raced away after the others. He'd waited just a little too long. Raider saw him arch his back in agony as a bullet reached him, but he managed to keep his saddle.

There was still considerable distance between the two groups. The bandits were able to make it to the cover of the boulders when the lawmen were still a hundred fifty yards away. Earp and the Mastersons seemed to be ready to ride right into the gully after them, but Raider had already noticed Hill and the others leaping down from their horses, taking up positions behind the boulders. "Hold up!" Raider shouted. "We're sittin' ducks out here!"

As if to illustrate his point, several rifles began firing from behind the boulders. Every man in the posse heard the meaty smack of the bullet that knocked Bill from the back of his horse. "Let's get us some cover!" Raider shouted.

Bill was half-sitting on the ground. The two Masterson brothers rode up to him, one on each side, grabbed him by the arms, then dragged him away toward the cover of a dry stream bed, while Raider and Wyatt provided a covering fire.

When they were sure that the Mastersons had reached safety, Earp and Raider turned and raced for the stream bed. They'd almost made it when there was another meaty smack, and Earp's horse screamed in agony. It managed to run another few dozen yards, but was beginning to fall as Earp ran it over the edge of the stream bed. The marshal had to kick his legs free of the stirrups and jump to avoid being pinned by the dying animal.

Raider rode into the cover of the little arroyo a moment later. He immediately dismounted, then led his horse into the deepest part of the arroyo, so that it would not be hit. After tethering the animal to a bush, he turned just in time to see Earp fire a pistol bullet into the head of his thrashing horse.

"How's Bill?" Raider asked, starting toward the wounded man.

"Dead," Bat replied. He'd been bending over Bill, trying to stop the blood flowing from his wound.

"Great," Earp muttered. "One man dead, my horse dead too, and Bill's horse nowhere around. No—there he is."

Everyone poked their heads up above the banks of the arroyo. Sure enough, Bill's mount, which had raced away in terror after its rider had been shot, was now munching grass off to the left, about two hundred yards away, closer to the bandits than to the possemen. "If I could just get to him," Earp muttered.

Apparently the bandits had similar thoughts. Two rifles roared from behind the boulders. Raider could see dust fly from the horse's flank. It threw up its head and screamed, then went down, legs thrashing. Earp cursed, then said, "Well, guess we'll have to go on in there, shoot those bastards all to hell, then ride their horses home."

"If we can get close enough," Raider replied. "They've got damned good cover."

Earp grunted in assent. Except for the posse's dry arroyo, and the gully that sheltered Hill and his men, the land was pretty damned flat. It would not be easy to get in among the bandits. "At least we can keep their heads pinned down," Earp said. He knelt behind the bank, pushed his rifle out in front of him, and began firing at the men behind the boulders. The Masterson brothers shrugged, then began firing too.

Raider went back to where his horse was tied. He opened his saddlebags and took out a box of Sharps ammunition. He began stuffing the huge cartridges into his pockets. Then he slid the big Sharps rifle from its saddle scabbard, and took it and the Winchester back to where the others were firing. There was a rock next to the bank. He went over to it, about ten feet from Earp, then took off his jacket, which he folded and placed on the bank in front of the rock. "Gettin' ready to take a nap?" Earp asked acidly.

Raider shook his shoulders, loosening his muscles. "Just

gettin' comfortable,'' he replied laconically. Then he sat on the rock and placed the forearm of the big rifle on his folded jacket, which made a nice steady shooting rest.

Raider was using a Sharps .45-120. It didn't have quite as heavy a bullet as the Sharps .50-95 or .50-100, but it packed a bigger powder charge, so that the bullet traveled with a little flatter trajectory. Still, it fired one hell of a damned big bullet.

Raider settled himself as comfortably as he could, cranked back the rifle's big side hammer, then pulled the set trigger. Now, the main trigger would go off at a touch.

He'd seen a puff of smoke coming from near one of the boulders. Slowing his breathing, Raider held the sights on the boulder. As he started applying pressure to the trigger, he held his breath. Even so, every time his heart beat, the sights jumped a little. He would have to fire between heartbeats.

As should happen during a carefully aimed shot, it was a surprise to Raider when the rifle fired. The butt slammed back against his shoulder, while a huge cloud of white smoke blotted out forward vision. Still, the bullet moved slowly enough so that Raider was able to peer through the diminishing smoke and see a puff of dust rise from the boulder where he'd been aiming. The sights were set just right.

"Damn!" Bat said, shaking his head, holding one hand over his ears. "Sounds like a cannon."

"Well, it ain't," Raider said morosely. "It won't bust up those rocks, and those buzzards are pretty well hidden."

"Yeah. We could be here all day."

Everyone nodded morosely. So far, it was a standoff. Both sides were well-hidden. Making a rush across such open ground would be suicide. "Maybe somebody should ride back to town, get help," Ed Masterson suggested.

"Then it'd be three against five," Earp said, shaking his head. "We might not be able to hold 'em there in those rocks."

"We've gotta cut their numbers down," Raider said.

But how? The bandits were keeping their heads down, and forcing the possemen to do the same by sending an occasional shot their way. An hour dragged by, then two. Then Raider got an idea. "There's one of 'em behind that big rock in the middle," he said.

"So what," Earp snapped. His temper was beginning to fray around the edges. "You ain't gonna shoot through that boulder."

Raider nodded. "Course not, but I think I can bounce a shot off of it, a little t' one side. Mebbe the bullet'll ricochet 'round b'hind t' where that yahoo's hidin'."

Bat grinned delightedly. "Like billiards."

Raider settled down to aim, judging angles. "Eight ball in the corner pocket," he muttered. The rifle fired. A second or two later, a faint scream came from behind the boulders. "Damn if it didn't work," Earp said grudgingly.

Now the bandits became more careful. There were not many targets. The day wore on. "It'll be dark in another couple of hours," Earp said. "Then they can just slip away."

Raider chewed his lip. "Yep. Guess it's time t' go git 'em."

Earp looked at him sharply. "You got a plan?"

"Yeah," Raider muttered. He'd been studying the terrain for the past two hours. "I figger two men on foot could crawl along this arroyo, then get into that other one, over there, and mebbe slip 'round b'hind 'em."

Earp rubbed his chin. "You may be right. Worth a try, anyhow."

A few minutes later Raider and Earp were on their way, crawling along the arroyo, sometimes on hands and knees, sometimes flat on their bellies. A bush screened them as they rolled out of their arroyo and into the shallow little stream bed that angled away from it. The second arroyo looped around behind the gully that held the boulders.

The light was beginning to fade. Raider realized that nightfall would help screen their movements as they approached the gully, but he had no intention of rushing into that gully in the dark. He pushed the pace, with Earp following right behind him. Within another few minutes they were only a few yards from the gully. They heard a single rifle bellow from among the boulders. "They haven't been shooting much," Earp whispered. "Maybe they're about out of ammo."

Raider made no reply, but suddenly stood up and walked quickly in among the boulders. Glancing over his shoulder, he noticed that Earp was right behind him. Then he turned all of his attention to the boulders ahead.

He was surprised when he saw no one at first; there should be five men sheltering among the rocks. They must be damned well hidden.

Then he saw a man, one of the hardcases Hill had recruited, lying behind a boulder. A rifle lay a couple of feet away. There was blood on the back of the man's shirt. Of course; he must be the one who'd been hit at the very beginning of the fight. Raider was surprised he was still alive.

There—another man. One of the Latins. He was poking his rifle barrel over the top of a boulder, apparently getting ready to fire again. There was blood on his clothing, too, low on his body. Raider looked around again. No one else was in sight, only those two, and the whole rear of the gully lay exposed in front of him. Where the hell were Hill and the other two Latins?

He started moving toward the two wounded men, hoping to get close before they spotted him and Earp. It was important to take them alive, to get them to tell him where Hill was.

But Earp suddenly sang out from behind him, "Throw down your guns, boys. You're under arrest."

The wounded hardcase looked around slowly, obviously too weak to move more quickly. The Latin spun with considerably more speed, although only his upper body did much moving. His rifle came around with him. Raider was aware of Earp, raising his own rifle, sighting on the wounded man. "No!" Raider shouted. But he was too late. Earp's rifle crashed. The Latin was thrown back against a boulder, his head a bloody mess.

Cursing, Raider ran to the wounded hardcase. He kicked the man's rifle out of his reach. He did not seem to have a pistol. The man looked up at him with apparent indifference, and then Raider was past him, running toward the man Earp had shot.

Dead. Dead as a doornail, with half his head blown away. He'd never get a word out of him now.

He walked back toward the wounded man, wanting to get there ahead of Earp, but there was no need to worry; Earp, as puzzled as Raider by the absence of any others, was cautiously poking his way among the boulders.

Raider knelt next to the wounded man. ''Can you talk?'' he asked.

The man looked at him blankly for several seconds, then his eyes cleared a little, focusing on Raider. ''Kind of,'' he muttered. His voice was so weak Raider could barely hear him.

''Where's Hill?'' Raider demanded.

''Huh?'' the man asked, obviously puzzled. He had apparently lost so much blood that he was barely functioning.

''Hill. The man who hired you for this job.''

A moment's blank incomprehension, then the man's eyes cleared again. ''That double-crossin' bastard,'' he muttered. A moment's hate flickered in his eyes. The hatred seemed to strengthen him. ''Left us here to die. Just me an' Miguel. A bullet smashed up Miguel's hips. Couldn't sit a horse. An' Hill, he didn't give a damn about me. Just took off ridin', with the other two. Just left us here to die.''

Raider glanced behind him. Yes, the gully deepened farther back. Men could have possibly led horses along it without being seen from the arroyo where the lawmen had been holed up. ''Where'd he go?'' Raider asked, although a terrible dread was growing inside him that he knew exactly where Hill had gone.

''Dunno,'' the wounded man said. His voice was weakening again. ''Said—he hadda take care of somethin'. I ast him to get me outta here. Wouldn't do it. Wouldn't even listen. After he and those other two left, I told Miguel we hadda give up. He said he'd shoot me if I tried. I—''

A spasm of pain twisted the man's face. his right hand clawed behind his back, toward his wound. He screamed once, then fell back, dead.

Raider was already getting to his feet. He heard Earp shouting to the Masterson brothers to come on in. Raider began to run, heading out onto the open ground in front of the gully. He saw that Bat was leading his horse. They met about fifty yards in front of the gully. Raider snatched the reins from Bat's hand, then leaped up into the saddle. He was pulling his horse's head around, when Bat called out, ''Hey—where are you going?''

"Town," Raider shouted back. "An' I hope t' God I ain't too late!"

Raider's horse was a good one, he'd picked it for its strength and endurance, but he nearly killed it on the ride back to town. The horse was lathered and panting by the time he raced down Front Street. It was growing dark. He guided the horse into the alley that led to Nanna's place. The horse was still moving when Raider's boots hit the ground. He took the stairs three at a time, pounding upward, calling out, "Nanna!"

There was no answer. He saw, to his horror, that the door to her room was slightly ajar. He pulled out his pistol and burst in through the doorway, his eyes frantically searching the room.

An oil lamp had been lighted, which at first gave Raider hope. He did not see Nanna; he saw only some words scrawled on the mirror behind Nanna's dressing table, painted in rouge. Just two words. "Traitor bitch!"

And then he saw her. Nanna was lying on her back, on the floor next to the bed, dressed in a peignoir, eyes open, staring up at the ceiling. There was blood on the front of the peignoir, right over her heart, and a lot more blood beneath her body.

Raider knelt next to Nanna, his pistol dangling from his hand. He pulled down the top of her peignoir. She had been stabbed, not shot. There was a bloody slit between her breasts. He quickly covered the wound; he could not bear to look at it.

Raider stared into Nanna's face, willing some sign of life to animate it once again. None did. None ever would.

Raider gently closed Nanna's eyes. She looked almost peaceful now. He remembered the dread that had filled her for the past few days. She had known.

Raider slowly stood up. He was surprised by how heavy his right hand felt. Looking down, he saw that he still held his forty-five. He raised the pistol, studied it, and as he did, his face hardened.

Benjamin Hill. Benjamin Hill had done this. Hill had to pay for his crime personally, had to pay the ultimate price. He'd find Hill if it took the rest of his life. He'd track him down and—

Standing above Nanna's body, staring at his pistol, Raider

swore a silent oath, a solemn promise to follow Hill to the ends of the earth, if that was what it took to find him. And there would be no question of bringing him in alive. He'd track the bastard down, and then he would kill him. Kill him as dead as Nanna.

Unless Hill killed him first.

CHAPTER NINE

After Bat and Wyatt returned to town with the bodies of the men who'd been killed in the fight, a concerted effort was made to find anyone who'd seen or heard anything concerning Nanna's murder. No one had. Raider figured Hill must have stolen into town from the back, killed Nanna, then left as carefully as he had entered. The next morning Raider tried looking for tracks leading out of town, but how could he possibly pick out the tracks of Hill and his men from the hundreds of others that had already scarred the ground?

Nanna was buried later in the day. Raider almost failed to attend the funeral; he did not want to hear any smarmy preacher's words spoken over her, insincere words, the canting of a hypocrite. But he finally went, and to his relief the only words said were friendly, sad words. Half the town had liked Nanna, admired her. The other half, the straitlaced half, had not even known she'd existed.

Their loss, Raider thought bitterly, as they lowered Nanna's body into a grave on Boot Hill. He'd have liked to have sent her body on to a better place, a place where she belonged, where she had family, but no one in town had the slightest idea where Nanna came from, where she might have folks.

So, Boot Hill it was, along with dead gamblers, cowboys, gunfighters, and whores. It wasn't until they were throwing dirt into the grave that Raider finally admitted that maybe this was just the way Nanna would have liked it; to be buried next to those she'd chosen to live among. She might even see it as a minor triumph over a society she'd obviously despised. Maybe. The only thing Raider knew for sure about Nanna was that she was dead. Just as dead as Hill was going to be.

Raider and the local law had already sent a number of telegrams to various agencies, listing Benjamin Hill as a very wanted man, wanted for murder and robbery. Hill's days of avoiding trouble with the law were over for good. Now, the nationwide information-gathering network of the Pinkerton National Detective Agency would be alerted. They'd be watching for Hill; there'd be eyes everywhere, from coast to coast. Not only Pinkerton operatives would be looking for him, but also thousands of eager volunteers: shopkeepers, druggists, cowboys, sheriffs, bank tellers, railroad ticket agents, a myriad of sharp-eyed individuals. Some would do it for the chance of earning a reward, others, because it gave them a vicarious thrill to be even this small a part of the country's leading detective agency, the legend, the Pinkertons.

On the other hand, Raider hated the thought of someone else collaring Hill. He wanted Hill for himself. He wanted to be the one to find him. The one to kill him.

He got his first break the next day. A dusty, dirty, tired kid of about twelve came stumbling into town on foot, looking for the law. Raider was in the marshal's office with Bat when the kid came panting in through the doorway. As soon as he saw the star on Bat's vest, the boy started blabbering. "Marshal—somebody done gone and stole our horses. Three of 'em. They—"

Bat got the kid to slow down a little and start from the beginning. With a little judicious prodding, they managed to get a clearer picture. At dawn the day before, three men had ridden up to the remote farm where the boy lived with his parents. They'd gone right to the corral and driven out the three horses that made up the major wealth of the hardscrabble little operation. The boy's father had run for his rifle, an old single-shot, muzzle-loading relic from the war. He'd managed to hold the robbers away from the house, but had not been able to save his stock.

"What'd they look like?" Bat asked.

The boy shook his head. "Couldn't get a real good look at 'em. Maw was tryin' to get me ta hide under the bed with her, but I crawled over to the winder an' peeked out. Maw fit to died, hollerin' at me to get back under the bed, but she's allus tryin' to make me do things I don't wanna do. There wasn't no way I was gonna miss that kinda—"

Bat sighed. "Kid, what'd they look like?"

The boy scowled at Bat for a moment; he wanted to tell the story his way; he wanted to relive every one of the feelings, the terror, the excitement he'd felt during the robbery. But he had a little trouble scowling into Bat's clear blue eyes. And the big man with the black hair and moustache, sitting just a few feet away, scared him more than just a little. "One of 'em was a dude," the boy blurted out. "City coat an' all. The other two was dressed a little different. An' they was kinda small an' dark."

Bat and Raider glanced at one another. "Could be Hill," Bat said.

"Could be," Raider replied laconically. He was already getting up from his chair. "Come on, kid," he said to the boy. "I want you t' show me where you live."

The boy was a little dubious. He'd rather have the man with the shiny badge take him back home. Boy, wouldn't that be something! However, half an hour later, he changed his mind when he saw the way the stranger was outfitted for the trail. He had enough guns strapped onto him and his horse to start a war.

The boy rode up behind Raider, with the butt of Raider's big Colt just inches from his own hand. Disappointingly, Raider said nothing at all as they rode out to the boy's place. It was a long ride; they didn't arrive until an hour or two before dark. It was a miserable little outfit; just a sagging shack for a house, another shack that was probably a barn, and a rope corral. The horses must have indeed been the place's only claim to wealth.

The boy's father was bitter. "Took me two years to save up to buy them nags," he muttered angrily to Raider. "Damn good animals. Those hombres—looked like their own horses was about played out. They coulda been a little more thoughty. They coulda left me their animals, even busted down as they were."

"They're not real thoughty people," Raider replied bleakly. "At least they didn't kill you."

The scrawny little man straightened his shoulders. "They tried. Lucky for them they got away. If I'd of had a repeater, well—"

He shrugged. "They was wanted men, I s'pose."

"Yeah," Raider replied curtly. Clearly, the man would have liked to ask more questions, but his Western pride kept him from poking and prying. He and his thin, wasted, half-starved, overworked wife asked Raider to stay the night, but Raider politely turned down their invitation. "Still be light enough for trackin' for another half hour," he said, and rode out of their dusty farmyard. The truth was, he had no intention of sleeping in either their house or barn. Both looked bug-ridden. He'd sleep out on the prairie, on the clean ground.

Raider rode out of the farmyard with the farmer's low-voiced cursing, bemoaning the loss of his horses, fading away behind him. For the first time since Nanna's death, Raider felt exultant, although it was tinged with bitterness. But now he knew he was definitely on Hill's trail; the farmer's description of the horse thieves, clearer than the boy's, had left no doubt in Raider's mind that it was Hill and his two remaining Latins who'd stolen the horses.

The trail was easy to follow, that of six horses, headed north across the prairie. The farmer had told him that one of his stolen animals was poorly shod. He'd even pointed out the mark made by the bent shoe on its right foreleg. "If you find em'," the man had said hopefully, "Maybe you could—"

Raider had promised to send the horses back. Along with Hill's head, he'd added silently. Uh-uh. He'd bring the bastard's head back himself, and personally lay it on Nanna's grave. She'd appreciate that. But of course, first he had to find them, find Hill. And survive the encounter.

Hill had a two-day lead on him. Fortunately, none of his horses seemed to be in as good condition as Raider's mount. He was certain that he could close the gap. They might not even know they were being followed. They might grow careless, they might lollygag along the way. But then again—

By the second day, Raider was beginning to grow optimistic. The tracks indicated that Hill's mounts, both the old ones and the stolen ones, were showing signs of tiring. On the morning of the third day, he saw smoke ahead. For a little while he thought it might be smoke from a fireplace or campfire, but as he drew nearer, he decided that it was not the right kind of smoke. It rose from too broad an area.

He was half a mile away when he realized that the smoke was coming from the remains of a burnt-out house. He could see a section of chimney sticking up from the ruins, in the middle of a farmyard. He rode in cautiously, looking for a possible ambush, but the terrain was too flat to hide much of anything, so he finally rode right into the yard, next to what was left of the house.

He almost immediately wished he hadn't. Two bloated buzzards were tearing at the remains of a body that lay about twenty feet from the house. Raider rode closer. The buzzards waddled away, apparently so gorged that they couldn't fly. Raider considered shooting them, but decided not to. The shot might alert someone close by, and the vultures were only doing their job, as revolting as it might be.

The body appeared to be that of a boy, perhaps twelve or thirteen years old. Despite what the buzzards had done to him, Raider could see that he'd been shot, more than once.

Movement behind some brush alerted him to another group of buzzards. This time he found the body of a grown man. He'd been shot, too. Raider rode around the yard, then saw that a small shed still stood, unburned, about fifty yards from the house. He rode over, pulling his Winchester from its saddle scabbard. When he was still a few yards from the shed, he saw bare feet sticking out of its sagging doorway.

He dismounted. Approaching slowly, he glanced quickly

inside. Two women lay on the floor of the shed. The one closest to the doorway had her skirt pulled up around her belly; she was naked from the waist down. There was blood between her legs, and more over her chest. The other woman was totally naked.

Raider lay his rifle aside and moved into the shed. He had to kneel. The woman nearest the door was dead. She'd been shot through the chest, obviously after being raped. The woman further inside was actually a girl. She couldn't have been over fourteen or fifteen years old. Maybe that's why they'd stripped her naked; she had a firm, lovely young body, what was left of it. She'd also been shot.

However, there was something about her color that alerted Raider to the fact that she was still alive. He quickly moved closer. Her eyes opened; she must have heard his movements. They were gray eyes. He watched as they flooded with terror. "No!" the girl moaned. "Don't hurt me no more—please."

"I'm not gonna hurt you, little lady," he said softly. "I'm here t' help."

The fear remained in her eyes for another few seconds, then was slowly replaced by a faint glimmering of hope. "Water?" she begged tentatively, as if testing him.

Raider raced outside, found a pump, and filled an old battered tin cup. He ran back to the shed, and knelt down by the girl. He was about to raise her head, then thought better of it. She'd been shot through the chest. Moving her too much might start new bleeding. He saw her clothes lying in a corner. Tearing a strip from her blouse, he soaked it in the water, then wrung it out into her mouth.

The girl's face cleared a little as she weakly swallowed a little water. "Thank—thank you, mister," she managed to say.

"What happened?" he asked. "Who did this to you?" He was pretty sure he already knew the answer.

The girl looked at him. She seemed to be having trouble focusing her eyes. Damn! She didn't look like she had much strength left. He looked at her wound, a bullet hole right in the middle of her chest. How had she managed to last this long?

"Three men," she said, in a strangely matter-of-fact voice.

''Stole our horses. Killed Paw an' Jamie when they tried to stop 'em. Then they took me an' Maw into the shed. They—did—things to us. Hurt us. Hurt us real bad. Maw screamed an' screamed. I—''

Her voice faded away. ''Then they shot us,'' she said, her voice blank. She suddenly looked alarmed. ''Maw! Is she—?''

She tried to sit up, to search for her mother. It was her last act. The movement seemed to break something inside her chest, some last strength that had kept her from bleeding to death. Blood gushed from her mouth, and she fell back again. Raider saw panic on the girl's face as she began to suffocate. He bent toward her, wondering what he could do, but it was too late. Already weakened, she died a few seconds later. He could see the light, the awareness, fade from her light gray eyes.

Raider spent the next three hours burying the entire family. The family murdered by Benjamin Hill and his two shadows. Nanna had told him how cold a man Hill was, how devoid of normal human feeling. Raider saw proof of that murderous coldness all around him, the burnt-out house, the dead father and son, the two raped and murdered women. He now had four more reasons to kill Benjamin Hill, four more reasons to stop him dead before he had the chance to create more scenes like this, the chance to hurt more people.

After he'd buried the family, Raider mounted his tired horse and started off once again on Hill's trail. The chances of catching him didn't look too good; Hill now had fresh mounts, he'd be able to make a lot better time. Raider was going to have to start taking it easier with his own horse; it was beginning to tire.

About a quarter mile from the burnt-out house, he found six horses standing, heads down, in a little draw, no doubt Hill's original three, plus the three stolen from the first farmer. They'd been ridden nearly into the ground. They hardly resisted as Raider rounded them up. He hazed them slowly across the prairie ahead of him. He knew they would slow him down, but it made him feel a little better, although he wasn't sure why.

Ten miles farther along, he reached a small town. He sold

Hill's three horses to the local livery stable. Part of the money went to buy himself a second mount, a hammer-headed, but otherwise likely-looking animal. He'd make better time now; he could change horses when the one he was riding got tired.

He found an honest-looking young man in the town's single saloon, and paid him twenty dollars to take the other three horses back to the farmer they'd been stolen from. Only then did he look up the local law, to tell him about the massacre ten miles out on the prairie. He'd purposely waited until the horses were on their way out of town; too many local lawmen would be tempted to impound the animals, then make a little extra money from their sale.

He only stayed in the town long enough to buy a few provisions, then once again he set out after Hill. However, he lost Hill's trail the next day. A large trail herd, no doubt on its way from Texas to Montana, had passed by. Hill had had the sense to follow in the herd's tracks. It was the first time Raider had seen the man take precautions. Maybe Hill was getting a little jumpy about possible retribution for the women he'd raped and murdered, the men he'd killed, the horses he'd stolen. Maybe it was beginning to occur to Hill that he could hang just as high as anyone else.

Raider had no choice but to follow the herd, trying his best to pick the spot where Hill and his men would strike out on their own again. That night it rained very hard, a real gully-washer. Raider huddled beneath his slicker for most of the night. When he crawled out into a bright, clear morning, and had a good look at the muddy ground, washed by runoff, he knew that there would now be no tracks for him to follow.

He could see a fair-sized town in the distance. He'd also passed telegraph lines a few miles back. It might be best to head into town, then telegraph the main office. Then the main office could telegraph operatives and lawmen in all the towns ahead of him to be on the lookout for Hill.

When Raider rode into town, he was mounted on his second horse; his big black was getting close to worn out. He felt dejected. Just a couple of days earlier he'd been certain he was going to catch up to Hill. Now he didn't have the slightest idea in which direction the bastard was headed.

His dejection made him careless, took his mind from his surroundings. He was swinging down from his horse, looking around for a telegraph office, when three men abruptly stepped out of a what looked like a hotel, about forty yards away.

Raider froze. It was Hill and his two men. They froze just as still; he could see Hill turn white. And then both Raider and the three men he'd vowed to kill exploded into action.

The fight started badly for Raider. His feet had just hit the ground. His horse, an ornery brute, was fiddle-footing away from him; he'd never have time to get his Winchester out of its scabbard, so he reached for his pistol.

Hill and the others were doing the same, but Raider reached a little faster. His intention was to shoot Hill first, then take on the others, but one of those little bastards was faster than a rattler, his pistol was already up and cocked, so Raider had to change his aim, drawing down on the quick little gunman.

Raider fired an instant before the other man, who staggered backward with Raider's bullet in his chest. The man's bullet went wild, hitting Raider's horse behind him, but by now Hill and the other Latin were firing, too. Water erupted from the watering trough next to where Raider had meant to hitch his horses. Another bullet knocked the hat from his head. He fired back quickly, too quickly; he hit nothing, but at least the blast from his pistol seemed to rattle the other two just long enough for Raider to dance backward.

Then a heavy blow struck his right leg. He knew he'd been hit, but even as he was going down, he was still firing. He saw Hill grab his shoulder, and spin halfway around. Then Raider hit the ground. He was aware of his horse, screaming in agony, going down next to him; he was afraid the animal might fall on him. As it was, the dying horse probably saved his life; it fell half in front of him, catching another bullet meant for Raider, which gave Raider a moment's grace during which he scrambled behind the water trough.

It was a big water trough; it gave a lot of cover. Raider was aware of a tremendous pounding in his leg. He felt giddy, but he dragged himself up and poked the muzzle of his pistol over the top of the trough. He hadn't been counting his shots, everything had happened too damned fast, but he knew he could not have more than another shot or two left. Damn, could he reach his rifle now?

Then he saw that Hill and his one remaining sidekick were running away, dodging back into the doorway from which they'd come. Raider snapped a last shot after them. The bullet tore splinters from the doorframe only inches from Hill's head; then he was gone from sight.

Raider heard a shout from farther down the street. Looking in that direction, he saw a man running toward him, carrying a shotgun. Sunlight glinted off a badge pinned to the man's shirt. That's why Hill had run, then; the local law was on the way. "Drop that gun, mister!" the lawman shouted, pointing the shotgun straight at Raider.

Raider obeyed without meaning to. His pistol seemed to slip out of his hand all by itself. Dizzy—he was so damned dizzy. Had he hit his head when he fell? Or was the wound in his leg worse than he'd thought?

The last thing Raider was aware of, before he slipped into unconsciousness, was the sound of two horses, somewhere near, being ridden away hard. Hill! He'd gotten away again!

Then—darkness.

CHAPTER TEN

Raider moved up the stairs slowly, leaning a little on his cane. He smiled, wondering how Bat would react if he could see him now; Bat had used a cane ever since he'd been shot by that army sergeant.

The leg was healing well. It had been a clean wound, with the bullet going right on through. It was loss of blood that had nearly done him in after the gunfight with Hill and his men; the wound had been a real bleeder. Fortunately, there'd been a fairly decent doctor in town. Raider had spent two weeks under his care. When he was able to move around on his own, he'd taken a train east, to the Chicago headquarters of the Agency.

The noise of Chicago's Fifth Avenue sounded behind Raider as he made his way up the stairs. He decided to try it without the cane; there were just a few more stairs. It hurt a little, but the leg seemed to be working again. He was pleased.

He stopped in front of a door. The words, "Pinkerton National Detective Agency," had been emblazoned on the door, surrounded by all kinds of curlicues and oak leaves. Under the name, a single open eye had been painted in. Beneath the eye was the motto, "We Never Sleep."

Raider opened the door and stepped inside a large office. Wagner, the office manager, was seated behind a cluttered desk. He looked up when Raider entered. "Good," Wagner said. "I've got a bone to pick with you, Raider. You're weeks behind on your case journal."

Raider fought down an urge to tell Wagner to go fuck himself. He hated paperwork. Even more than paperwork, he hated criticism from a desk man. "Is the Old Man in?" he asked curtly.

Wagner pursed his lips. He appeared to be about to make some tart rejoinder, but he correctly read Raider's mood, and backed off. "Yes. He's expecting you. Go on in."

Raider nodded, then moved toward the door to an inner office, the Old Man's lair, the office of the founder, Allan Pinkerton himself. Raider knocked. An unintelligible growl came from the other side of the door. Raider opened the door and stepped inside.

No matter how tough he tried to be, no matter how relaxed, he was usually shaking in his boots when he entered the Old Man's office. This time he was simply shocked. The Old Man looked terrible, wasted, shaky. He'd had a stroke several years before, a crippling stroke, but Raider had heard that he'd recovered. He must have had another. His hands were shaking, his face was thin and pale, there was something wrong with his mouth. But apparently there was nothing wrong with his mind. "I know, I know," the Old Man said gruffly. "I look like something the Devil spit back out. Getting old's no damn fun, Raider."

.He looked at Raider's cane, then glanced at his leg. "Tell me how you managed to get yourself shot, then let your man get away."

Raider flushed. He remembered the gunfight, how he'd let himself be surprised. He should have checked the town out before riding straight in. He should have been on his guard every moment. Had it been fatigue, or had it been a single-minded desire for revenge that had made him so careless?

He told the Old Man about the case, how they had set up

Hill, how Hill had gotten away after Wyatt Earp's decoy made a mess of things. He told him about tracking Hill into Nebraska, about the massacred family, and about the gunfight.

Pinkerton shook his massive head. While his face might be wasted, his skull was still large. An Old Testament beard still sprouted from his chin. Even sick, he was a formidable man. "Tsk, tsk," he said. "You should have called in more men. You shouldn't have gone after Hill on your own. But you lost sight of a lot of things because of the woman, didn't you?"

Raider started. How had the Old Man know about Nanna? Might as well ask how God knew what time of day it was. "I made some mistakes," Raider admitted.

Pinkerton nodded. "You got yourself very involved, laddie. I should take you off this case, do you know that? I should put someone on it who doesn't have his emotions all riled up."

Raider nodded reluctantly. He had indeed made a hash of things. He was surprised, then, when the Old Man cleared his throat, then said, "But I won't. If you have any brains, you'll take the way you feel and use it. Use it to get Hill. You will get him, won't you?"

Raider had been ready to quit, to resign his job with the Agency, then go after Hill himself. He wanted Hill badly, and he wanted him dead. But going after him alone would be a forlorn hope. After the gunfight, Hill had seemed to disappear. A lone pursuer would be at a terrible disadvantage. But now, with all the resources of the Agency behind him—"Yes. I'll git 'im," he promised, nodding his head.

Pinkerton nodded back. He looked tired. "Good. Tell Wagner what you need. And take care of that leg."

The Old Man nodded his dismissal. Somewhat surprised, Raider turned around and headed for the door. Usually, every time Raider came to Chicago, Pinkerton would spend at least five minutes chewing him out for failing to write daily reports, for spending too much expense money, for his drinking, gambling, and whoring. The fact that he hadn't done any of this suggested to Raider that the Old Man must be even sicker than he appeared. Raider glanced back over his shoulder. Pinkerton was leaning back in his chair, eyes closed. His face looked like death itself. He must have sensed Raider's hesitation. His eyes opened slowly, found Raider, then initiated a scowl that slowly moved all the way down his ravaged face. "What the hell are you waitin' for, boy?" he growled. "Go out and get the bastard!"

Raider stepped through the door, closed it behind him. He met Wagner's eyes. For once the office manager didn't try to look at him disapprovingly. His eyes mirrored Raider's concern for the Old Man. "He can still think," Wagner muttered lamely. "He's still the best."

Raider nodded. Allan Pinkerton had been the best for most of his life. Born in Scotland, he'd attracted the unfavorable attention of the British authorities while still quite young. He had been a labor agitator. He left Great Britain a hop, skip, and jump ahead of the noose, migrating to Chicago.

Chicago and its environs had been wild and woolly at that time, back in the late forties. Like the British, the Americans had always had an aversion to uniformed, regular police forces. The populace feared having a police state forced on them, the kind that existed in Spain, France, and Germany. Only the county sheriffs, often either corrupt, or incompetent, or both, and privately hired watchmen, guarded the peace. Crime abounded. Footpads, robbers, and bandit gangs terrorized the nation.

With a Scotch eye for opportunity, Pinkerton had seen the glaring need for competent law enforcement. After personally apprehending some desperadoes, usually alone and unarmed, Pinkerton had founded his detective agency. From the first, he meant it to be run on sound scientific principles. His operatives were trained to be precise, ruthless, and relentless. A strict code of conduct had been drawn up. These were all regulations that Raider hated, but they worked. Maybe, Raider thought, if he'd followed standard procedure a little more closely, Hill would be swinging from a rope right now. And maybe Nanna would still be alive.

The sound of Wagner clearing his throat broke Raider from his reverie. "What do you need?" Wagner asked.

Raider looked up. "I think I better spend some time in the gallery."

• • •

The files of the Pinkerton National Detective Agency, the
rogues' gallery, was a massive collection of old and new reports, case journals, and more importantly, photographs. Allan
Pinkerton had been one of the first men in law enforcement to
appreciate the value of the relatively new art of photography.
As photographic equipment became more efficient and porta-
ble, operatives were encouraged to carry cameras with them
into the field and to photograph everything connected with a
case, even the corpses of dead bandits.

It was these photographs that most interested Raider. He'd
already plowed his way through mountains of cross-indexed
information, and had found nothing at all on Benjamin Hill.
He'd checked any records that even faintly referred to the
wartime Kansas border raiders. Still no mention of Hill.

So he turned to the photographs. There were thousands of
them. There was nothing to do but begin searching through
them, one by one.

The photographs had not all been taken by Pinkerton operatives; indeed, most had not. The Pinkertons had discovered
some time ago that many desperadoes had an almost childlike
urge to be photographed, so when operatives were working a
case, they visited all the photo studios in their area of opera-
tions. A small gratuity would usually encourage a photographer
to show them copies of the pictures he'd taken. Any photographs bearing, even tangentially, on current, or even old cases,
were purchased, then sent on to Chicago and the main office.
These dusty, fading pictures were currently Raider's main hope
for hunting down Benjamin Hill.

Of course, reward posters had already been sent out, coast
to coast, offering, under the familiar logo of the unsleeping
eye, a reward of one thousand dollars for the apprehension,
dead or alive, of one Benjamin Hill. But Hill's description
could fit many men, and no doubt he'd changed his name by
now; Hill was no fool. Raider's main hope lay in the photographs.

Days passed. Raider's nasal passages became inflamed from
inhaling old dust. He took a break every afternoon to walk the
streets of Chicago, strengthening his leg. He hated cities, and

particularly hated Chicago, which was growing with malevolent speed. He hated the noise and bustle of it, the lack of open ground. The people were too damned pushy; their pushiness would get them a belly full of lead in some of the places Raider had been.

On the eighth day, Raider found what he was looking for. He was by then so bleary-eyed, so sick of pictures, that he almost put the faded old photograph back in its file without really looking at it closely.

But something caught his eye. He held the photograph up to the light. It showed a young man, dressed the way eastern city dudes used to dress twenty years ago when they headed West. The young man wore a brace of Army percussion Colts and a big hat. The hat partially shaded his face, which was the reason Raider had almost passed it by, until the eyes had caught him. Even shaded, they showed the same cold nothingness he'd noticed in Hill's eyes the first time he'd seen him in that saloon in Dodge City.

He studied the photograph more closely. Yes, it had to be Hill. He began to pull papers out of the file in which he'd found the photograph. James Gates. That was the name in the file. The picture had been taken in the California mother lode country, during the time of the gold rush, back in the early fifties, more than twenty years earlier. Raider read on. James Gates had been wanted for robbery and murder. He'd been part of, or maybe even the leader of a gang that specialized in robbing and murdering miners. The rest of the gang had been killed or captured and hung. Gates had managed to get away. He'd never been heard of again.

By God, he'd been heard of now. Raider was positive that James Gates was Benjamin Hill. Or the other way around. Either way, one rope would put an end to both names.

Within a couple of days, hundreds of copies of the old photo had been made and disseminated to sheriffs' offices and police forces all over the United States, along with the new name, James Gates. Maybe somebody out there would remember a bandit named Gates.

Raider was not about to merely sit and wait. Less than a week after finding the photograph, he was on his way west, headed for the mother lode country, armed with a dozen copies of the old photograph. And a relentless desire to find his man.

CHAPTER ELEVEN

Raider shifted his butt on the hard seat. He was growing bored; hell, he'd been bored for two days. Looking out the train's window didn't help much; the land went by too damned fast for him to really appreciate it. Particularly traveling across the prairie. There wasn't much you could see on the prairie, not at a glance. You had to be riding a horse, or, God forbid, on foot; then you could see all the little things that made the prairie so interesting: the small animals burrowing through the buffalo grass, a patch of flowers fighting their way toward the sun, and, of course, the wind, the feel of it, the smell of the land that it carried to you.

The only smell in this damned train was of unwashed bodies, when the windows were closed, and of soot when they were open. That, and an aching butt. How the hell had they managed to make these seats so damned hard?

Still, if you were in a hurry, you couldn't beat the train. Not unless, someday, men learned to fly like the birds. And Raider was in a hurry; he wanted to get out to California as quickly as possible, to start digging for information on Hill. Or should he think of him as Gates now? James Gates.

Hill would do for the moment. Hill was the name of the man who'd killed Nanna. That name was going to sound in Raider's head until he'd destroyed the bastard.

He hardly expected to find Hill in California, but the gold rush country used to be his stamping grounds. Maybe there would be people there who remembered him, knew things about him that would lead Raider in his direction. It had been his experience that hunted men tend to move in patterns. It would make more sense if they'd completely break their old patterns, shy away from everything they'd ever done before, anyplace they'd ever been, but the human animal did not seem to work that way. Fugitives tended to look up old friends, return to familiar places. Maybe it was the very act of being a fugitive that made them do it. Maybe being on the run engendered in a man the need for something familiar, for the consolation of imagined normalcy.

Of course, Hill might be different. Raider remembered the lack of feeling in the man's eyes. Maybe he'd just vanish.

Raider wondered if Hill had much money. He'd had money in the bank in Dodge, and of course, he'd owned a lot of property. But Hill had been forced to leave Kansas so quickly that he'd been unable to get his money out of the bank, or convert his property to cash. Maybe he was broke. The way he'd stolen horses while fleeing Kansas might indicate that. Or maybe it was simply Hill's viciousness that had prompted him to steal, rape, and kill while he was rounding up remounts.

Raider drummed his fingers on the wooden train seat. Hard as hell. He looked around at his fellow passengers, then wished he hadn't. Bunch of dudes. Hell, ten years ago, a trip to California would have taken a man weeks, maybe even months, depending on how many other people he was dragging along with him. Now, it was a matter of four or five days. You didn't need any guts at all to make the trip. The West was going to fill up with soft, spoiled Easterners, with all their pettifogging rules. Pretty soon you'd need a license to walk down the street.

Raider kept up pretty much the same train of thought for the next couple of days. He didn't particularly like thinking this way, but if he kept his mind filled with trivia, he was less likely to think about Nanna. Less likely to remember her dead, staring eyes. What hurt most of all was his memories of her alive, making love to him, laughing, maybe scolding her dance hall girls. Even the memories of her awful depressions reminded him that he had once known Nanna as a living, breathing person, and that he never would again. The final image that always stuck in his mind was of that obscene knife slit in her breast.

Two days later, still in pretty much the same mood, Raider watched the world black out as they went through an enormously long tunnel. This was the final barrier before the descent down the Sierra slopes into California. It was a warm day, the windows were open. The rackety-click of the train's passage bounced off the tunnel walls into the car. Then they were through, and passing along the edge of a very high cliff. A deep canyon yawned to the side. One good rock fall, and they'd go over.

Like everyone else in the car, Raider did not start breathing easier until they were past the chasm. It wouldn't be long, now. Raider looked around at his gear. His saddle and other horse furniture were in the baggage car, but he'd insisted on bringing his rifles with him. The Eastern passengers had looked askance at the rifles, but none had had the balls to say anything. Maybe they figured he was local color.

His railroad pass had stilled any opposition from the railroad people. The Pinkertons did a lot of work for the railroads. Hell, they were still chasing the James gang all over the West. Not very successfully, true, but the Pinkerton National Detective Agency was the railroads' best bet for keeping the line at least partially free of train robbers, so each Pinkerton operative had a permanent, free railroad pass. Second class, of course. No point in letting the troops get uppity ideas about their own importance.

A couple of hours later, the train dropped down into the enormous San Joaquin Valley. An arid place, but with incredibly fertile soil. The valley ran four or five hundred miles, north to south. Just a few years ago they'd started irrigating the land. Raider saw immense farms, stretching away for miles, out of sight. The valley was so wide that a person could only see its edges on a clear day.

By nightfall they were in Sacramento. Raider retrieved his gear from the baggage car, then hired a wagon and driver to take him to a hotel. Sacramento was a bustling, busy town, the state capital. It was also the terminus for the river traffic plying the network of deep-water rivers that ran down from the mountains, through the delta, and into San Francisco Bay.

Tired from the train trip, Raider eschewed the town's bars, and went to bed early. The next morning he toured the local livery stables and stock auctions, looking for a horse. By afternoon he'd found a likely candidate, a big black, pretty much like his last horse. The animal had spirit; it tried to bite Raider, but he cuffed it lightly, and the animal began to get the idea that maybe he'd finally met a man who could handle him.

Like most Westerners, Raider had no romantic notions about horses. They were transportation, absolutely necessary transportation, given the vast distances one had to travel in the West. If you had to ride a horse to death to get where you needed to go, then you rode it to death and got another one.

Still, only a fool mistreated his mount. Sometimes your horse was the only thing that stood between you and death, whether you were in the process of running from a bunch of hair-hungry Indians, or plodding across a desert looking for water. Raider treated his mounts well, unless his survival needs said otherwise. You could always find another horse—if you were still alive.

Raider left Sacramento the next morning, before dawn. He spent the first half of the day getting used to his horse, and getting the horse used to him. There were a few tense moments when the horse pushed to see just what it could get away with. Absolutely nothing. When the horse had made sure of that, it behaved well enough.

Raider made camp early that evening, while it was still light, next to a stream. After making certain that his horse was securely tethered to a tree, he fired his pistol for a while, studying the animal's reaction. The first couple of shots startled the animal; Raider saw it's eyes widen, and its nostrils flare. It tugged against the rope, but not in complete panic.

Raider walked over to the nervous animal, and spoke softly to it. He moved the pistol close to its muzzle, so that it could smell the gunsmoke, get used to it. The horse snorted, but Raider's casual attitude toward all this noise and smell seemed to reassure it. Raider spun around and blasted away at a rock near the stream. The horse shifted nervously, but did not tug at the rope. Raider nodded, satisfied. The big black would probably behave well enough if a gunfight developed.

By the middle of the next morning, Raider was starting up into the Sierra foothills. The original gold strikes had been farther toward the valley, but they had soon played out. Most of the gold had been found in stream beds. As it was panned out of the lower streams, the miners had pushed higher into the mountains, toward wherever the source was.

According to the Pinkerton dossier, Hill/Gates had not shown up in the placer mining districts until well into the fifties. Twenty years ago. The dossier had no information on where he'd come from. That's what Raider hoped to find out.

That night he made camp in a mountain meadow. He liked these mountains, although they were as cold as hell in the winter. He could have stayed in a town, but he preferred to make camp in the grass. Now that most of the placer gold had been taken, many of the towns were abandoned, or nearly abandoned. Weeds grew up through boardwalks in front of impressive, deserted buildings. Most of the real gold now lay to the east, in Nevada. The Comstock Lode. Virginia City. Deep, hard-rock mines that ate miners alive every day, as they slaved away in the stifling depths far, far away from light and air.

There were still settlements here, there were still people; the area was simply too beautiful to abandon completely. Raider began making his rounds, showing the old photograph of Hill/Gates. The reception he received was usually cold, until he mentioned the thousand dollars reward, but no one seemed to recognize the man in the picture, which was not surprising. Most of the men who might have known Gates would have moved on long ago, chasing their gilded dreams.

After two weeks, Raider was thinking of giving up. Maybe it'd be better, he thought, if he rode on down to the cities.

Someone may have responded to the wanted posters. Maybe Hill had already been found.

He was on his way down the mountain when his horse threw a shoe. He tried to hammer the shoe back on with a rock, but most of the nails had been lost. It wouldn't have mattered much, if the ground hadn't been so rocky. By noon, his horse was noticeably favoring its shoeless hoof, the right front.

Raider dismounted and began leading the animal. His feet soon began to hurt like hell; the high heels and narrow toes of his boots made walking painful. He considered opening his saddlebags and taking out the moccasins he kept there. Damned rocky ground, though, and his feet were soft from wearing boots too long.

Then he saw smoke ahead. He read it as smoke from a chimney. Sure enough, another hundred yards along the trail he came around a bend and saw several cabins nestled under some huge Douglas firs.

As he walked toward the cabins, he made certain that his right hand was close to the butt of his Winchester. You never knew—

He saw, as he drew closer, that most of the buildings were abandoned. Only one cabin and a couple of outbuildings showed any sign of use. The smoke was coming from the cabin's chimney.

Raider knew better than to walk right up to a place. Anybody who lived way out here might be just a little bit jumpy. "Hallooo the house!" he sang out.

A moment later a shaggy head thrust out through the cabin's open doorway. Raider could see the muzzle of a rifle just below the head. It was a gray head, with a tangle of hair and beard. Beady little eyes glittered somewhere between the masses of hair. "Who might you be, stranger?" the man asked.

"My horse threw a shoe."

Still, there was just the head of the rifle muzzle protruding from the doorway. Raider held up the shoe. "Got any horseshoe nails?" he asked. "Maybe a hoof hammer?"

Now the man came out of the doorway into the open. Raider saw that he was very skinny. His clothing was ragged, but clean and serviceable. The rifle was an old percussion Civil

War Springfield. "Yeah, I got tools," the old man said. At least, Raider figured he was old. It was hard to tell, with all that hair.

The man was still suspicious, but Raider suspected that a longing for company was beginning to overcome the man's caution. He walked up to Raider's horse, still lugging the old rifle, which was just about as tall as he was. After looking down at the horse's hoof, the man said, "Yeah, we can fix that up easy enough."

He looked up at Raider, and now there was hope on his face. "You wouldn't happen to have a drop or two in them saddlebags, would ya?"

Raider grinned. "Reckon I might."

He opened the saddlebags and took out a half-full bottle of whiskey. The old man licked his lips. Up this close, Raider could see that he must be close to seventy. Raider handed him the bottle. The old man's face was a study in fascination as he pulled the cork. Tipping the bottle to his lips, he threw back his head and swallowed greedily. The level in the bottle diminished with amazing speed.

The old man took the bottle away from his lips. Raider saw a shudder shake his skinny frame. "Needed that," the old man said. He started to hand the bottle back to Raider. Raider shook his head. "Keep it," he said.

The glee in the old man's eyes suggested that Raider had made a friend for life. Remembering how the old man had sucked on the bottle just a moment ago, Raider expected him to drain it dry. Instead, he went over to a rough pine table near the cabin's door, and reverently set the bottle down. "For cold and lonely nights," the old man said softly. Then he turned toward Raider. "Now, let's fix up that horse o' yours."

The old man was garrulous as only a lonely man can be. His name was Zeke; he gave no last name. He chattered away as he worked on the shoe, pounding it out straight before he nailed it into place. He would not let Raider help. As he worked, he gave a little of his history. He'd been living in these mountains ever since the old gold rush days. "Beautiful up here," he kept repeating. "Too bad all the folks went away. Most of the gold played out. I pan the stream over yonder."

He looked up anxiously, as if he'd given too much away. "Hardly any real color," he added quickly. "Make just enough to keep myself in beans and bacon."

By now the shoe was in place. The horse was looking bored; it wanted to drop its head and browse on the thick grass that grew near the water trough. Raider thanked Zeke. He was about to mount up and ride on, when he remembered why he was here. Zeke was an old-timer. He might just—

But Raider was not prepared for Zeke's reaction, after he'd pulled out the faded old picture of the young man with the crossed gunbelts, and showed it to the old-timer. Zeke just glanced at it at first, and was about to hand it back, when he suddenly jerked it closer to his face, and took a hard, searching look. "Why, it's that son of a bitch, Jim Gates!" he shouted.

Raider's eyebrows rose. Jackpot. "Did you know him?" he asked hopefully.

"Know him?" Zeke replied indignantly. "Why, the bastard tried to shoot me!"

"And you've remembered it all these years?"

Zeke looked at Raider as if he'd lost his marbles. "All these years?" he snorted. "What the hell are you talkin' about, mister? It was only a little more'n a week ago."

CHAPTER TWELVE

Raider was, to put it mildly, stunned. He wondered if the old man was more confused than he looked. However, when Raider questioned Zeke about what he'd just said, he stuck by his guns. He waved his arm vaguely toward the north. "Happened over that way, couple of miles up in the hills. Son of a bitch nearly cooked my goose. An' it wasn't the first time. Twenty years ago—but maybe I better start at the beginnin'."

Clearly, Zeke was eager to tell a tale. That was fine with Raider. In all the wash of words, there might be nuggets of information about Hill.

Zeke moved over to the table, where he sat down on a section of stump that served as a chair. There was another such chair on the far side of the table. "Park your butt," Zeke said. "I cut me that damn thing in case I ever had a guest. Now I do, so don't let it go to waste."

Zeke's eyes strayed toward the whiskey bottle, which was only a few inches from his right hand. He hesitated; then, after muttering, "Oh, what the hell," he pulled the cork and took a drink, just a sip this time. Then he leaned his elbows on the tabletop.

"It was way back in fifty-four," Zeke began. "That's when I first met Jim Gates. He was just a kid, maybe in his early or middle twenties. Arrogant bastard, even way back then. He run around like King Shit, in that fancy outfit o' his, hung with guns. Mean. Real mean. I saw him kill some poor little bastard one night. The man got drunk an' mouthed off a little to Gates. Well, Gates just pulled out one o' them Colts and killed the fucker. Shot him dead. The other man had a gun, but didn't have much idea how to use it. That was like Gates; go after the weak ones, step soft around anybody that might fight back."

Zeke took another sip of whiskey. He licked his lips, then smiled. "I was one o' the ones that fought back. I never was much for talkin' a whole lot, back in those days. Guess you'd never believe that now. Never showed off my gun, neither, kep' it in my coat pocket. Well, one day Gates started in on me, tryin' to rile me. I told him what an asshole he was. He kinda went white around the gills, but there wasn't much he could do right then; we was in a saloon, an' it was full o' my friends. He left, kinda smokin' from the top of his head. Ev'rybody figured that was that, but not me. I knew he'd be alayin' for me, so when I left the place, I was real careful.

"Sure enough, I spotted him behind some trees. He pulled out one o' those Colts the minute he seen me. Took him too long to open up, though. Like I said, I didn't go around sportin' my gun. I figure he thought I didn't have none, so he took his time; just enough time for me to pull out my smoke wagon and open up."

Zeke chuckled, slapping his leg. "Oh, that was comical. I can't shoot for shit, but bullets was knockin' bark off trees all around Gates. He got off a shot or two, then ran. Just lit outta there like his tail was on fire. Disappeared back into the trees. Laugh? I thought I was gonna die laughin'."

Zeke took another sip from the bottle. When he put it down, Raider expected him to start talking again, but the old man just sat there, staring off into space, back through the years. "And that was all?" Raider prompted.

Zeke shook his head. "Huh? Well, I figured a snake like

Gates wasn't gonna take that too well. He'd be layin' for me. I knew I was gonna have to watch my back. The son of a bitch mighta got me eventually; he was a real back-shooter. Or he mighta hired somebody; he always seemed to have money, though he didn't seem to do anything to earn it. Didn't pan for gold, didn't do a lick o' work. We figured he musta had money of his own.''

Zeke chuckled. ''Turned out it was other people's money. We'd been havin' trouble with a gang o' thieves. Nasty bastards. They used to kill the people they robbed, so's they couldn't talk, I s'pose. Well, one day this gang—it turned out to be four of 'em—was holdin' up a coupla miners headin' down inta the valley with their gold. Lotta gold. What those varmints didn't know was that there was another group ridin' about a mile behind, a dozen men. Well, they rode right inta the robbery, just in time to see those night-crawlers gun down the two miners. This new batch was well armed, an' they opened up on the bandits. Killed one of 'em outright, an' wounded another so bad he couldn't ride. The other two got away. If they'd o' had any brains, they'd o' kept right on ridin'. But I guess maybe they figured both o' their buddies, the ones who got shot, had died right away, before they talked. Wasn't the case. Before he died, the wounded one, I figure he was pissed off 'cause he figured the other two had left him to die, gave the posse the names o' the two who got away. And damned if one o' those names didn't belong to my old friend, Jim Gates.''

Zeke chuckled again. ''Well, he wasn't gonna sneak up on me now. Ever'body in these mountains was out lookin' for him. Sneaky bastard, though. When the posse caught up to the two of 'em, Gates managed to slip away again. He was good at that.''

Raider nodded. Hill/Gates seemed to have a talent for getting out of tight spots, usually by sacrificing the men he was riding with.

''But they got the other one,'' Zeke said. ''All shot fulla holes, but still breathin'. An' talkin'. Guess he was religious, or somethin'. He knew he was gonna die, but he wanted to die clean. Kinda shriven, I 'spose. Anyhow, he cursed Gates a little, then said as how he an' Gates had buried all that gold they'd lifted off those two murdered miners. He was gonna tell the posse where they buried it, even described the general area, but the son of a bitch went an' died 'fore he could give too many details.''

Zeke chewed his lip a little. "Musta been twenty or thirty thousand worth o' gold involved. Maybe more. Well, most of us knew, from what the dead bandit had said, more or less where the gold was, within a coupla miles. But up here in these mountains, a coupla miles can cover a lotta possibilities. I'll tell ya, there were men diggin' in every badger hole for miles. No way Gates coulda got in there to dig up the gold. He was lightin' out, anyhow. Somebody spotted him the next day down in the valley. Then he just disappeared. Nobody never saw the son of a bitch again, till I spotted him a little more'n a week ago. Boy, didn't that kinda make my hair stand up and take notice.''

"Where'd you see him?" Raider asked. If Hill was in the area, he wanted to get after him right away.

"Comin' out of a little lodgin' house down toward the valley. Him an' a Mex. For a little while there, I thought these tired old eyes was playin' tricks on me, but damn if it wasn't Gates. Those eyes o' his, ya know. A man never forgets—''

Zeke shook himself. "Well, I ducked back outta sight 'fore he saw me. He an' that Mex was headin' for their horses. An' damn if they didn't have shovels tied onto their saddle bags. I knew, then, that Gates was on his way to dig up that gold, the loot he'd buried twenty years ago. Guess he figured nobody'd recognize him now. He didn't count on me. I had a lot of reason to remember the bastard.

"Anyhow, I had my mule near. An' old Betsy, here." Zeke pointed toward his rifle, which was leaning up against the door frame. "So I followed 'em.''

"Alone?"

Zeke grinned sheepishly. "Yeah. I wanted that gold for myself. If I hadn't o' been so damn greedy, I woulda ast some o' my friends to go along. But I didn't, an' I got nothin'. Nothin' at all.''

"They saw you," Raider said.

Zeke shook his head. "Not right off. I followed 'em for miles, staying well back. You see, we all knew the general area where the gold was, but not the exact spot. So I hung back, even circled around 'em. And, by God, when I saw 'em again, they were diggin'! Diggin' up the gold!

"I stayed hid until they'd finished. I saw Gates and that Mex pull some sacks outta the ground. The sacks was all rotten. They poured the gold into some new sacks they'd brought along. Sure was shiny; I could even see it from where I was hid. That's when I made my play. I figured I could drop Hill with old Betsy, an' maybe the little Mex would get scared off, ride away without the gold, or at least leave plenty behind. But when I was sneakin' up on 'em, damned if I didn't step on a stick. Guess I was so het up an' excited by the sight of the gold, that I started actin' like a fool. Gold can do that to a man. Anyhow, they both turned around. I had old Betsy ready to rip, an' I shot, but by then it was too late. They was both runnin' for cover.

"Then it was my turn to run. Old Betsy's single shot. I had to hunt up some cover while I reloaded. I ducked back into a little ravine, an' started pouring powder as fast as I could.

"They didn't panic. The Mex kept me pinned down while Gates was stuffin' bags fulla gold. I got off a shot or two, enough to keep 'em from sneakin' up on me. Then the Mex shot my mule. I heard 'em ridin' away a few minutes later. Not much I could do about followin' 'em, me bein' on foot. Damn, I hated losin' that mule!"

"And you didn't say anything to anybody?"

Zeke grinned sheepishly again. "Nope. Too damned embarrassed. Made a real fool outta myself, droolin' after the gold that way. Up here, in the old days, I saw many a man ruined by that kinda greed. Figured I shoulda learned better in my old age. Don't know why I'm tellin' you all this now. Maybe it's the whiskey."

Zeke held up the bottle and looked at it. "This Devil water has ruined more good men than gold ever did. But I sure do like the stuff."

He uncorked the bottle and took another sip.

Both men were silent for a while. "All this happened about a week ago?" Raider finally asked.

"Yep."

"And you haven't seen either Gates or his man since?"

"Nope. Figure they lit out. They had the gold, didn't they?"

"And no idea where they went?"

"Nope."

The conversation lagged a little. Finally, Raider figured it was time to ride on. He doubted it would do much good, but he asked Zeke for directions to the lodging house where he'd first seen Gates. As Raider mounted, he told Zeke that he'd try and send him part of the reward money, if his information helped locate Gates. Zeke shook his head. "Hell—I already lost the gold. I ain't countin' no more chickens till I can see feathers."

The lodging house was ten miles down the mountain, a rambling structure of logs and planks. It had probably done very well twenty or twenty-five years earlier, when the area had been swarming with gold-seekers. Now it had an air of neglect and poverty.

The lack of guests made it easy for the man running the lodging house to remember Hill. But he either didn't know a damned thing, or he wasn't talking.

Raider took a room, on the off chance that he would meet someone who knew more than the proprietor. The room smelled musty and the bed sagged, but at least the food was good; the owner had shot an elk the day before.

Nobody seemed to know a thing about Hill. He'd only stayed at the lodging house long enough to get his bearings and buy the shovels. He had said very little to anyone. "Well, he did talk to that Mex he was with," a man told Raider, "but they was always jabberin' away in Mes'kin'. I couldn't understand a damn thing."

Raider decided to leave the next day. At least he knew that Hill had been this way. He'd probably head down toward Sacramento or San Francisco. Maybe people along the way would remember him. He'd have to use the picture again.

He got a break sooner that he expected, while the lodging house's hostler was saddling his horse. The hostler was a Mex-

ican. "Señor," he said to Raider. "I unnerstan' you are lookin'
for thees hombre who was here a few days ago. This Señor
Weelson."

Wilson was the name Hill had used. He sure as hell seemed
to have a lot of names. "Yeah," Raider replied.

The hostler looked around nervously. "The rest of these
cabrónes, they don't know nothing. They don't pay no attention. But this Weelson, he talk to me like I am dirt under his
feet, an' the man with him—he was no Mexican, señor—he
treat me like I am dirt, too. So I listen when they talk in Spanish.
I listen to them argue. The gringo, he wanna go to Los Angeles.
The other one, he keep sayin' he wanna go home. But he never
say where home is. But it is not Mexico, señor."

Raider thanked the hostler and gave him a dollar. The hostler
grinned hugely. "You are after this man?" he asked. "He has
done something bad? You will hang him?"

Raider nodded. "If he lives that long."

The smile broadened. "Good. Any man who treats Juan
Dominguez like dirt should hang."

Raider mounted his horse and rode away. He turned once.
The hostler was still standing there. He waved, his smile still
in place. Raider nodded. Benjamin Hill Gates Wilson sure had
a way of making enemies.

CHAPTER THIRTEEN

Raider immediately headed down the mountain, toward the valley. It sounded like Hill had more than a week's lead on him. That might not matter. Hill did not know his next destination had been overheard by a despised hostler. Of course, since Zeke had spotted Hill digging up the gold, he might be a little jumpy. He might keep on heading south into Mexico, where it was easy for a man to disappear.

When Raider reached Sacramento the next day, he discovered that the rails had finally been built all the way to Los Angeles. The first through train had left only a few weeks earlier. Raider was on the next train out. This time he took his horse with him, in the train's livestock car. Before the train left, he took the time to send a cable to the Chicago office, alerting them to the possibility of Hill's presence in Los Angeles.

Of course, it was only a possibility. Perhaps Hill's sidekick had finally convinced him to return home, wherever that was, which could be anywhere. Even if Hill had gone to Los Angeles, it might not be easy to find him. And even if he found him, it might be hard to do anything about it. Los Angeles, like most of the rest of Southern California, was a lawless place, ruled by a mob of drunks and criminals. It was a good place for a man on the run to go to ground.

The train rattled south at the blistering speed of nearly thirty miles an hour. At this rate he'd be in Los Angeles tomorrow. Raider leaned back in his seat, watching mile after mile of land roll by outside the window. Where there was no water, the land was sere and bare. Where irrigation had been used, crops grew in amazing abundance. The soil, having been washed down from the mountains over immense periods of time, and never before used for agriculture, was incredibly fertile.

The further south the train traveled, the more arid the land became, until it approached true desert. On the morning of the next day, the train began to climb up the Tehachapi Loop, a long, sinuous grade of switchbacks that took the track up into the mountains that separated Los Angeles from the great valley to the north. The land was tremendously rugged, and, once again, at least at the lower elevations, very dry. Finally, the tracks descended a steep pass into the great San Fernando Valley. One more pass through a range of hills, and the Los Angeles plain lay ahead, a flat brushy terrain stretching to the sea, thirty miles away.

Raider had not been in Los Angeles for a while. The old Spanish pueblo was in obvious transition. True, there were still large numbers of long, low adobes, with their tile roofs, but there were also many modern buildings. After he'd had his horse taken to a livery stable, along with his saddle gear, Raider carted his bedroll and rifles away from the train station. The Pico House hotel lay straight ahead of him. He debated taking a room there; he'd heard on the train that the Pico House had hot water on each floor and gas lighting. It was supposed to be the fanciest hotel south of San Francisco. It might be nice to get himself a good room; he still had enough of his card winnings from Dodge to afford it. On the other hand, he might stick out a little in such a fancy place. He sure as hell didn't want to draw Hill's attention, if he was indeed here, until he was ready for him. His leg throbbed as he remembered his last unexpected encounter with Hill and his men.

So Raider took a room in a small place in Sonora Town, where most of the Mexicans lived. The owner's wife, a fat woman of about fifty, who was at least ninety percent Indian, brought him a jug of water and a basin. Raider spent the next ten minutes scrubbing off some of the soot and cinders he'd picked up on the train trip.

There was a small Mexican restaurant next door, just the front room of an adobe house, outfitted with some rickety tables and chairs. There was nothing at all rickety about the food. Lots and lots of chili. Perspiring heavily from the food's spiciness, Raider repeatedly cooled his mouth with swigs of beer that was, thank God, at least somewhat less than body temperature. God, but he loved Mexican food!

Clean and fed, he set out into the town to look up an old friend. He'd left his rifles behind in his room, but he was packing his Colt. Unlike Dodge City, there were no gun rules in Los Angeles. There were many armed men on the streets.

And much use of weapons. Raider heard a hoarse shout coming from the open doorway of what looked like a saloon. A moment later a man came flying backward through the doorway. He fell in the street on his back. Raider could see that he was bleeding; he'd been badly cut on the arms and face. A moment after the man hit the street, another man appeared in the doorway, holding a long, bloody knife. He glared down at the fallen man, seemed about to come out after him, then he cursed under his breath, turned, and disappeared back into the saloon. No one made a move to help the fallen man. He slowly staggered to his feet, streaming blood, then staggered away. Toward a doctor, Raider hoped.

Raider had gone only another block when he heard the sound of gunfire from a back alley. It seemed to bother no one.

A couple of inquiries brought him to the house of the man he was looking for, Maj. Horace Bell. He'd known Bell some years before, when Bell was a Texas Ranger. Raider knew that there was little use in talking to the local sheriff; the lawmen in Los Angeles, like the judges and mayors, were elected by the mob of drifters and fugitives who populated the place.

But Horace Bell was a man of rectitude. He'd help, and he'd be a lot more help than most men. Bell maintained very good relations with the Mexicans and Californios, who still made up a sizable chunk of the local population. A lawyer by trade, Bell did his best to protect Los Angeles's Latin citizens from the greed of the Yankee newcomers.

Bell himself met him at the front door of his house. He was a man in his middle forties, quite tall, at least as tall as Raider, and ramrod straight. He had an enormous moustache, under piercing eyes. It took a moment for Bell to recognize Raider, but when he did, he smiled. "My God! What brings you here? What a pleasure. Come on in."

As Raider walked in through the door, he noticed a heavy Colt pistol lying on a small table right next to the door. Among his other activities, Major Bell ran a newspaper, *The Porcupine*, which was a prickly a publication as its name implied. Bell used the paper to verbally tear the hide off the corrupt local politicians. A lot of men would like to see Horace Bell dead.

The next half hour was spent in general conversation, as each man caught up with the other's activities. Bell had quite a history. He'd been a gold miner up north, when he was not yet twenty. Later, still very young, he'd been a California Ranger, hunting the notorious Joaquin Murieta. Still looking for adventure, he'd become an officer and aide in the rather dubious army of the filibuster, William Walker, conqueror of Nicaragua. During the Civil War, Bell had been a Union officer, and later, a Texas Ranger. All his life, Horace Bell had been a man of action. He had not modified his fearlessness, even in Los Angeles. For several minutes, Bell talked about local corruption. "Place was okay back in the fifties," he groused. "Then, when the war started, it filled up with a bunch of Southern sympathizers, the kind who were willing to shoot a man in the back if he was for the Union, but not the kind who had to guts to go east and join the Confederate army, where somebody might shoot back. White trash. They're still here; they're still back-shooters."

Eventually, the talk moved to Raider's reason for being in Los Angeles. Bell listened to his tale of Hill's depredations.

"And you think he's here?" Bell finally asked.

"Good chance. The question is, how do I go 'bout findin' 'im?"

Bell thought for a moment. "Let me see what I can do," he finally replied. "Lend me a few of those photographs. I'll go to some of the old families, find out if they, or their men, know anything at all. It may take a few days."

Within an hour, Raider was back in his room. He spent most of each day inside, going out at night to eat. There was no point in warning Hill that he was in town. On the evening of the third day, a young Mexican boy knocked on the door of Raider's room. Breathing a little fast, probably excited by this wonderful whiff of intrigue, the boy told Raider that Major Bell wanted to see him.

Raider went straight to the ex-Ranger's house. Bell got right to the point. "I think we've found your man," he said. "He's staying at a ranch up near Sepulveda Pass—if you want to call it a ranch. Den of thieves would be a better word. He's in with the Smith brothers. I gather they're protecting him. Did you expect him to have those kinds of connections down this way?"

"He's got money."

Bell nodded. "That'd do it. The Smith brothers would sell their own mother if the price was right. You ready to ride?"

Raider's eyebrows rose. "Ride?"

"Of course," Bell snorted. "To take a look at the place. Make sure that it's really your man hiding out there."

So, the old war horse wanted in on the action. Why not? "I'll get my horse," Raider replied, grinning.

They were on their way within twenty minutes, accompanied by the same boy who'd brought Raider the message. Raider smiled a little as he looked over at Bell, who was riding an enormous black stallion, accoutred in Spanish horse gear from a generation ago; heavy, hand-tooled saddle, with silver mountings, fancy silver bit with a bosal, and a big rifle stuck into a hand-tooled leather scabbard. Major Bell, wearing a flat black hat, and dark clothing, was every inch a warrior, half Anglo, half Latin.

It was quite dark by the time they reached the mouth of

Sepulveda Pass. They carefully approached a ranch house situated about half a mile west of the pass, along the lower slopes of the Santa Monica Mountains. Dismounting in a gully, the three men walked on foot to the edge of the gully and studied the house. Light spilled from several of the windows, none of which were closed; it was a warm night.

"I don't see any dogs," Bell whispered. "We can get a lot closer."

"Don't need to," Raider replied. He'd brought his binoculars. He began studying the house. Several men were sitting outside on a rickety porch, next to a lamp, drinking and playing cards. There was movement inside the house, too. Raider could not tell how many men were inside.

A man came out of the front door. Raider stiffened. Bell sensed his excitement. "What is it?" he hissed.

"Not sure," Raider whispered back. He was studying the man who had just come outside. The light was not good, but he was pretty sure it was Hill's sidekick, the mysterious Latin who wanted to go home.

A moment later he was sure. Hill himself came to the door. Standing in the doorway, where the light was good, he called something to the Latin, who turned and went back inside with Hill. "It's them, all right," Raider muttered, loudly enough for Bell to hear. "But now what? There's just too damned many men down there."

Not only were there a lot of men, but they appeared to be heavily armed. Every man seemed to be wearing a pistol, and several rifles leaned against the house's front wall, close to the door. These were clearly hard men. To go after Hill by himself would be suicide.

Raider lowered his binoculars. "Let's git outta here," he said.

They worked their way back to their horses, mounted, and started back toward Los Angeles. "What now?" Bell asked, after they'd ridden a couple of miles. "The Smith brothers have a lot of backing around these parts. The sheriff and the mayor owe them a lot. You won't be able to raise a local posse to go after your man. If you try, you may find yourself in more hot water than the man you're after.''

"I know," Raider replied. "That's why I'm gonna send a telegram as soon as we get back t' town. In a few days, Benjamin Hill is gonna find hisself facing men he cain't buy.''

CHAPTER FOURTEEN

Three days later, Raider and Major Bell were at the train station as the train chugged in. Amid clouds of steam and smoke, a dozen hard-looking men descended from one of the coaches. One of them, a big man with a drooping walrus moustache, spotted Raider. He led the others toward Raider and Bell. Hands were extended, but no one really smiled. "Glad to see you could make it here so fast, Jones," Raider said dryly.

Jones nodded. "McParland said to get here fast. What have you got for us, Raider?"

"A killer. We're gonna have t' wade through a few hardcases t' git to 'im."

"When is this gonna happen?"

"Right now. Or he'll be warned, and light out. He's the hardest man t' catch I ever seen. Every time you think you got 'im, he kinda squirts out from under your thumb."

Jones nodded again. "We'd better get the horses down, then."

Some of the men were already heading back toward the live-stock cars. Within a few minutes, a dozen big horses were being led down ramps. Some of them shied a little as the train's engine vented steam, but most held steady. Well-trained horses. The mounts of men who fought for a living.

It took twenty minutes to unload all the horses, get them saddled, and put all the weapons in place. Each man had at least one rifle. Some had shotguns. And every man carried a minimum of one pistol. Of course, as they pulled gun belts from valises and buckled them on, and slipped rifles into saddle scabbards, they could not help but attract attention. Nervous citizens edged away. When they were finally ready to ride, Raider saw the sheriff come huffing along the street, heading straight toward them. "What the hell's goin' on here?" the sheriff demanded.

Raider looked coolly at the man. Many sheriffs were corrupt. The Los Angeles sheriff was famous for his corruption. "Goin' huntin'," Raider said dryly.

"Now, see here," the sheriff blustered, but Raider and the others were already swinging up into their saddles. Raider looked down at the sheriff. "We'll bring you some o' whatever we catch," he said flatly, then pulled his horse around.

The others followed, including Major Bell, who rode up alongside Raider. He looked around at the heavily armed men. "Pretty hard looking bunch," he observed quietly.

"Yeah," Raider replied. "If we cain't outshoot Hill an' his bunch, mebbe we can scare 'em t' death."

A light smile tugged at Bell's lips. "I think we'll have to outshoot 'em."

Raider, Bell and the dozen gunmen rode straight out of Los Angeles, heading west. When they'd left the town behind them, Raider called a halt. He explained to Jones and the others who they were after, and what kind of opposition they might expect. "These Smith brothers may be blowhards, or they may be real tough hombres," Raider said. "We'll try t' take 'em by surprise, ride in hard, an' git it over with quickly. Remember: we're basically after two men."

Every one of the twelve posse members nodded. Raider nodded back. McParland had picked his best. All twelve men belonged to the other side of the Pinkerton National Detective Agency. These men were enforcers, not detectives.

They reached the area near the Smith brothers' ranch house late in the afternoon. In another half hour it would begin to grow dark. As before, Raider stopped in the little gully that overlooked the ranch house. Taking his binoculars, he, Jones, and Major Bell moved cautiously into place on foot. The ranch house lay below. Raider put his binoculars to his eyes, scanned the yard. When he brought the binoculars down, he looked worried. "Hardly anybody down there," he muttered to the others. "Mebbe they're off somewhere else. Sure wouldn't wanna hit the place, then find out Hill isn't even there."

"Hey," Jones cut in. "Somebody's coming."

Sure enough, they could hear the sound of hooves off to one side. A moment later two men rode into view, one riding a bay, the other a big white stallion. Raider stiffened. "That man," he murmured to Jones. "The one on the white horse. He's the man we're after."

Sure enough, Hill and his sidekick were riding into the ranch yard. Raider watched both men dismount, then tie the reins of their horses to a post next to a side window. Hill and the Latin walked around to the front door and went into the house. Jones nudged Raider. "You're sure that's your man?" he asked.

"Yeah. Positive."

"Then let's hit them now, before one of our horses whinnies and gives us away."

"I don't know," Raider murmured back. "Makes me downright uneasy, with so few men down there."

"You sure do look a gift horse in the mouth," Jones snorted. "This is gonna be a cakewalk. We just ride right in there and take your man. With the odds so much in our favor, there may not even be any shooting."

Raider was still nervous; he sensed something wrong. But then one of the Pinkerton horses did whinny. There were three men in the ranch yard. Raider saw one of them look up suspiciously. "Okay," Raider snapped. "We hit 'em."

Raider, Bell, and Jones ran back to where the others were waiting, and quickly mounted. Raider waved the men forward. "Go in hard, boys. Don't give 'em a chance t' put t'gether a defense."

The fourteen men came pounding out of the gully, every

man with a rifle or shotgun ready in his hands. However, it was already a little late. That whinnying horse had alerted the men in the ranch yard. As the posse came thundering into view, still about a hundred yards away from the house, the three men were racing toward the porch, where their rifles were stacked. Two of them ran into the house. The other turned and brought his rifle to his shoulder. Several of the Pinkertons fired first, and the man was driven back against the front wall of the house, his shirt showing a number of bloody holes.

It still should have been easy. Even with armed men inside the house, they would not yet have had time to put together a coordinated defense. The Pinkertons were riding in fast, ready to dismount the moment they reached the house, and thrust rifles into every window and door.

They did not get the chance. Raider heard a loud cry from about a hundred yards behind them, followed by several shots. Twisting in his saddle, he saw, to his horror, half a dozen men riding hard toward the posse, every one of them shooting. His nervousness was now justified; it was the rest of the Smith brothers' gang, coming at them from behind.

Raider remembered then, Hill and the Latin riding up to the house. They must have ridden ahead of the main group. He should have thought of that. Too late to cry over spilled milk now; nothing to do but fight like hell.

Raider heard a bullet strike the Pinkerton next to him. The man grunted, then slid from the saddle. However, the Pinkertons did not panic. Raider heard Jones bellowing for three men to take shelter behind a shed and open up on the six men racing toward them. Meanwhile, four other Pinkertons opened up on the house, shattering windows, blasting splinters off doorframes, and in general doing a good job of making the men inside keep their heads down.

But the most important problem was to defend themselves against the six men riding toward them. Raider shouted an order, and four Pinkertons rode out to the side, looping around to the right of the bandits, making them split their fire between this new attack, and the three men sheltering behind the shed.

Then Jones and two other men rode straight toward the bandits, standing in their stirrups to give them more stability as they poured fire from their Winchesters into the outlaws.

With fire coming from the three sides, two of the Smith brothers' gang went down immediately. Another reeled in the saddled, clutching his side. That left only three unhit.

And now Jones and his two men were on top of them. Raider saw one of the Pinkertons knocked from his saddle by a bullet, but the other two had closed now. Jones tossed his rifle away and fired his pistol point-blank into the bandits, hitting one. The remaining Pinkerton yanked a sawed-off shotgun from his saddle and blew away another.

Meanwhile, Raider had stayed behind, near the house. He was currently the only one watching the house. The horses Hill and his Latin had ridden up on had panicked. They were tugging at their reins, but were too tightly tied to escape. Then Raider caught a flicker of movement from a window. A moment later he saw a figure, half-hidden by some bushes, slip from the window and jump up onto the back of the big white stallion.

Hill! It had to be Hill. Raider was certain he recognized the hat the man was wearing, and the way he moved. And it was Hill's horse. The white stallion reared under the weight of the rider, then raced around toward the back of the house. Raider immediately raked his horse's flanks with his spurs, and took off in pursuit, but he had to swing wide of the house, to avoid being shot by the men cornered inside. When he came out into the open the white horse was a quarter mile ahead.

Dusk was falling, it was growing a little difficult to see, but the white stallion stood out clearly against the darkening landscape. Raider urged his horse onward, but the white stallion was a fine animal; it was maintaining its lead over Raider's mount.

The two riders raced over the brushy ground. Raider worried about gopher holes, rocks, anything that might trip or slow his horse, but there was nothing he could do about it, no way he could be careful without losing Hill, so he pushed his horse onward, recklessly.

It was Hill's horse that stumbled. Raider saw the animal falter for a second, then it resumed running. But Raider was sure that the animal's speed had slackened a little. Either it was hurt, or whatever it had stumbled over had frightened it.

Raider began to close with the other man. In the growing gloom, he saw the man turn back to look at him. He caught a glimpse of white face. Go ahead, Hill, Raider thought triumphantly. Keep looking back. Slow yourself down.

By now the stride of Hill's big stallion was noticeably off; the animal had obviously hurt itself. Raider began to close more rapidly. The other man was aware of it. Once again Raider caught a glimpse of a white face peering back at him through the gloom. Worry, Hill, Raider thought exultantly. Worry about what I'm going to do to you.

Suddenly the horse swerved toward a tangled patch of cactus and rocks. The white horse ran right up to the cactus, but stopped before entering the patch; the way in was too narrow. Its rider dismounted, then ducked in among the cactus.

Raider immediately dismounted, too. He could no longer see Hill; it would be easy for Hill to shoot at him from where he was hidden.

Raider took cover behind some rocks, while he studied the cactus. Most of it was four or five feet high, of the broad-bladed fleshy variety, each leaf two or three feet long, and a foot wide. The entire patch covered an area perhaps twenty yards across and thirty yards long. The cactus had grown up so thickly that there was no way to see inside the patch.

There was a lot of open ground between Raider and the cactus patch. He wished he could tell just where Hill was hiding. Maybe the best way would be to show a little of himself. He cautiously poked his head up above the rocks in front of him.

Hill's reaction was more than Raider cared for. Two closely-spaced shots roared out from inside the patch. One bullet knocked his hat from his head, the bullet itself traveling hotly maybe half an inch from his scalp.

But he had seen where the shots were coming from. Levering his rifle rapidly, Raider fired half a dozen shots into the cactus. He heard a yelp from inside the patch. Even before the echoes of his shots had faded away, Raider was in motion, running toward one side of the patch.

He halted right at the edge of the cactus. A solid wall of

broad, pulpy leaves faced him. He could not see past them at all.

Raider froze in place, half-kneeling, trying to quiet his breathing. Maybe if he couldn't see Hill, Hill couldn't see him. But he sure as hell didn't want Hill to hear him, either.

Hill was obviously playing the same game. Raider could not hear a sound from inside the patch. It was now a cat-and-mouse game. But who was the mouse, who was the cat? The first man who moved was going to be a target. Raider decided to fake it, make the other man think he'd moved.

He looked around him. A round stone, about the size of his two fists together, lay next to his right foot. Bending cautiously, afraid that his joints might crack and give him away, Raider slowly picked up the stone. When he had it in his hands, he tried to figure the best way to throw it without giving his position away.

He shot-putted it, so that it crashed into the cactus about ten yards to his right. Almost immediately gunshots crashed from inside the patch, three fast shots that tore the hell out of the cactus around where the rock had struck.

Now, from the sound of the shots, Raider knew where his man was hiding—about ten feet straight ahead of him. Rising up onto one knee, Raider fired ten shots from his rifle, fanning them out in an arc, all around where he'd heard the shooting coming from. The roar of his Winchester half-drowned an agonized scream from inside the patch, but Raider was sure he'd heard it. He stopped firing. His ears were ringing, but now he heard a soft, sobbing moan come from inside the patch. "Oh, God," he heard a voice murmur.

Was it a trick? Was Hill in there just waiting for him to come and investigate?

The only way to find out was to go right on in, go in fast. While the cloud of powder smoke from his rifle was still surrounding the place from which he'd fired, Raider stood up, then ran, crouching low, toward the point at which Hill had disappeared into the cactus patch. Cactus spines tugged at Raider's clothing, lacerating his skin. The barrel of his Winchester kept getting hung up on cactus leaves, so he dropped it and drew his pistol.

He found his man a few feet farther along, lying in a pool of blood. Cactus leaves, while large, are soft and fleshy, not good at all for stopping bullets. The man had been shot all to hell. The trouble was, it wasn't Hill.

"Who the hell are you?" Raider snarled as he knelt beside the man, checking quickly to make certain he was not holding a weapon.

"B-B-Billy," the man stammered, through a froth of blood that bubbled from his lips. He stared up at Raider, his eyes wide with fear. Then he died.

Cursing, Raider looked down at the man. His hat was lying right next to his body. It did look a lot like Hill's hat, the same pearl-gray felt, the same flat brim. And he was more or less Hill's size. Raider cursed himself for putting too much together; the hat, the white horse, which he'd watched Hill ride up to the ranch house, and most of all, his own desire, his rage, his need to get Hill. Even if it wasn't Hill.

Raider backed out of the cactus patch, picking up a few more spines along the way. His horse was standing patiently a few yards away, cropping a tuft of coarse-looking grass. Raider swung up into the saddle, then raced away toward the ranch house.

As he neared the house, he could hear firing, which meant that the fight was not yet over. The firing was desultory, though, which probably meant some kind of standoff.

It was now almost completely dark. Raider had the sense to slow his horse when he was within a hundred yards of the shooting; he didn't want to get blasted from the saddle by a nervous Pinkerton. "Jones!" he shouted.

"Who's that?" Jones's voice shouted back.

"Raider. I'm comin' in. Hold your fire."

Following the sound of Jones's voice, Raider rode toward a stand of brush that stood on a low rise, about seventy-five yards from the front door of the ranch house. It was the closest cover to the house itself. As he rode into the brush, he saw flame blossom from one of the house's windows. A moment later a bullet sang by his head. Damned good shooting in this light.

It was very dark in the brush. A form moved toward Raider. "Jones?" he asked.

"Yeah. Saw you ride off a while ago. Did you get your man?"

"Uh-huh. But it wasn't the man I was after. What's been happenin' back here?"

"Nothing much. Those six yahoos that charged us? We settled their hash real good. Four dead, with the other two wounded pretty bad. Trouble is, by the time that particular fight was over, the people in the house had pretty well covered the yard. We tried a rush, but their fire was just too damned hot to stand up to."

"How many of our men got hit?" Raider asked.

Jones hesitated a moment. "One dead. Two wounded pretty bad, another two with scratches."

Raider nodded glumly. Like most efforts to nail Benjamin Hill, this one was not going at all well. "Where have you got the men posted?" he asked.

Jones pointed to dim shapes hidden in the brush. "Three right here, covering the front door. Sent the rest of the men around to the back and sides, so nobody can get out of the house."

"Unless they can slip away in the dark," Raider muttered.

"I don't think so," another voice said, from his left. Raider turned. Major Bell was standing a couple of feet away. "Moon's coming up," Bell said. "Nearly full. It'll light that yard up almost like it was daytime. Nobody's gonna sneak out of that house. Nothing but open ground all around it."

Raider looked to the east. Sure enough, a fat, shining moon was just breasting the Santa Monica Mountains. Its silvery light was already beginning to illuminate the ranch yard. Raider studied everything he could see. Bell was right. In every direction, there was at least fifty yards of bare dirt surrounding the ranch house. "They might not be able t' sneak away," he said bitterly. "But by the same token, there's no way we're gonna sneak up on that place without gettin' our asses shot off."

"I wonder what the hell we can do?" Jones murmured. Raider realized that he sounded a little unsure.

"First thing is to take care o' the wounded," Raider replied.

"We're gonna havta send a man into town t' hire a wagon so we can haul 'em back to a doctor."

Jones nodded. He seemed more positive as he detailed a man to ride back to Los Angeles and hunt up a livery stable. But after the man had ridden away, there was less to be positive about. Raider, Jones, and Bell made a slow, careful circuit of the house, searching for any cover that would permit a man, or men, to work their way in close. There appeared to be no possibilities. Each wall of the house had at least one window, from which all possible approaches could be covered. There were no ditches, no brush, no outbuildings. Any man either crawling or dashing across that fifty yards of open ground in clear moonlight would be riddled before he'd gone halfway.

Raider spent the next hour making certain that Jones's men were positioned as well as possible. They were to fire occasional shots through the windows and the single front door. There was no point in firing at the walls; they were made of thick adobe.

A little after eleven, the man who'd been sent into town returned driving a flatbed wagon. He'd had the foresight to stock it with a number of blankets. The wounded men were placed in the back of the wagon, cushioned by blankets. Other blankets were torn up to improve the dressings covering their wounds.

The wagon was about to leave, with two men accompanying it, one to drive, the other to see to the wounded, when Raider had a sudden idea. "Hold up," he said. He turned toward Major Bell. "Where can we get our hands on some dynamite?"

Bell thought for a moment. "Stores are all closed. But I know a man who'll open up for us if I go along and talk to him personally."

So Bell rode away with the wagon. That left the Pinkerton posse thin on the ground. Raider and Jones walked another circuit around the house, making sure that all avenues of escape were closed. "How many d' you think are in there?" he asked Jones.

"Four or five. Just enough to cover each side of the house."

There was nothing to do but wait. Raider and Jones decided to have their men stop firing. "Don't make a sound," the men were told. "Maybe they'll think we got discouraged and left."

But the men in the house were not that foolish. Although they too stopped firing, there was no sign at all of movement from inside. Were they waiting for reinforcements?

Raider was beginning to wonder if maybe all the men inside were dead. Then he heard the sound of a wagon and team, moving toward the ranch yard. After a few minutes of tension, it was discovered to be the wagon that had taken the wounded into town. Major Bell was riding alongside. "We got the dynamite," he told Raider, when he was close enough to make out faces.

Raider realized that it was slowly growing light. They'd wasted the whole damned night. Bell went to the wagon, and produced an entire wooden crate of dynamite. "We'd better disperse it," Raider warned. "If one lucky shot from the house hits that box—"

The dynamite was dispersed to safe points that could not be hit by gunfire from the house. It was fully light by the time Raider was ready to use the dynamite. Apparently someone inside the house saw movement. A rifle fired, and bullets cut brush near Raider's head. Everyone hunted better cover.

The problem was, how to get close enough to the house to use the dynamite? One of the Pinkertons, a huge man with apelike arms, was posted at the point that came closest to the front door. A fuse was attached to one of the dynamite sticks, then lighted. Under heavy covering fire, the man ran forward twenty yards, drew back his arm, and threw. The dynamite arced through the air, while the man raced back toward cover. There was a shout from the house. Probably the sight of the dynamite sailing through the air was the only thing that kept the retreating Pinkerton from being hit, as the defenders inside the house ducked.

The dynamite exploded fully ten yards from the front door. With the force of the blast uncontained, all the explosion accomplished was to raise a big cloud of dirt and dust. The house appeared unscathed.

Raider knew that they'd never be able to repeat the maneuver. The defenders would be on their guard now. They'd shoot down anyone who broke cover. Raider eyed the house's thick adobe walls. "We've gotta get close enough t' throw some dynamite in through the door or a window," he told Jones and Bell. "But how—?"

The answer came to all three simultaneously. "The wagon!"

It took the better part of an hour to turn the wagon into a miniature fort. An old barn, a hundred yards from the house, was torn apart to provide lumber, which was then nailed into place around the front and sides of the wagon, to protect the man throwing the dynamite.

The sun was well up by the time they had finished. Raider decided he'd do the throwing. The wagon tongue was lashed into place, so that the wagon would roll straight. Raider climbed inside, hoping the boards nailed into place would be thick enough to stop bullets. Taking several sticks of dynamite, complete with fuse and blasting caps, he settled into place, his rifle close at hand.

Four men got behind the wagon, then started pushing it straight toward the house's front door. As soon as the wagon broke cover, furious fire lashed at it from the house. Crouched behind the layers of boards, Raider heard bullets striking inches from his body. None penetrated the wood.

The wagon crept across the yard. From inside the house, the defenders tried shooting beneath the wagon, to hit the legs of the men pushing it, but skirts of heavy planking hung nearly to the ground. Nevertheless, it seemed like hours to Raider before one of the men called out from behind him, "You're only ten feet away!"

Raider popped one eye above the boards. The door lay just ahead of him. Ducking, he lit one of the sticks of dynamite. With the fuse sputtering, he popped up again. If he missed, if the dynamite hit the doorframe and bounced back under the wagon, he'd be blown up.

The stick of dynamite sailed right through the doorway. He heard a shout of fear from inside. Would they throw the dynamite back out? Into the wagon?

This was no time for what ifs. Raider was already lighting another fuse when the dynamite went off. The blast was partially muffled by the thick adobe walls. The entire doorframe was blown outward, smashing into the wagon. Part of the roof lifted off, tiles flying every which way. A wall partially collapsed.

Raider was already rolling out of the wagon, with a sputtering stick of dynamite in his right hand, his rifle in his left. He raced around the side of the building, sticking close to the wall, heading toward a side window. He glanced at the dynamite in his hand. God, but the fuse was short!

Reaching the window, he tossed the dynamite inside, then fell to the ground. The explosion was almost instantaneous. Dirt and debris blew over Raider, but fortunately the wall did not blow out and fall on him.

Raider leaped to his feet. The window frame was a ragged hole. He thrust his rifle inside, and began firing as rapidly as possible. After several shots, he leaped in through the window, immediately flattening himself against the wall. The dust was beginning to clear. He saw what looked like a man, or most of a man, lying close to the opposite wall. The dynamite hadn't left much.

Raider moved to the interior doorway. He could hear Pinkertons coming in through the front door. He heard several shots, followed by a scream. He moved through the doorway, calling, "It's me, Raider, comin' out."

By now the house was full of Pinkertons. They moved from room to room. One of the bandits, hidden in a room on the far side of the house, tossed his rifle into the hallway. "Don't shoot! I'm comin' out!" he shouted.

The only other man inside the house still alive was Hill's Latin. Raider found him in a back room, unconscious, but still breathing. He'd been hit twice. Both wounds had been bandaged. From the dried, crusted blood on the bandages, he'd been wounded early in the fight.

There was no sign of Hill. Raider searched the house carefully, looking for trapdoors, but the floor was made of tiles laid down on packed earth. Hill was nowhere to be found.

"Hey, Raider!" a voice called. "The greaser's conscious."

Raider rushed into the back room. The Latin was indeed conscious, but only barely. Raider knelt next to him. The man's eyes slowly focused on him. "You!" the man murmured in Spanish. "Always you."

"Where's Hill?" Raider demanded. At the sound of Hill's name, the man slowly shook his head. "A bad man—bad luck for me and my brothers," he groaned hoarsely. "We will never return home now. The only one who will get there is the man you call Hill—Don Enrique—*Mal hombre—mala suerte.*"

The man's eyes closed. Raider knew he'd die soon; he wondered how he'd survived this long. "Home," he prompted. "This home you talk about. Where is it? Where is home? Where is Hill goin'?"

The man's eyes slowly opened. "*Mi país,*" he said softly. "New Granada. Panama. My brothers—"

Panama? He was from Panama? Raider began another question, but the glazed look in the man's eyes told him he would not get an answer. He watched the last of the man's life fade from his eyes, the last of his consciousness. There would be no more information.

He'd called Hill Don Enrique. Henry. The man had more names than a small city. Raider wished the dead man had had time to mention Don Enrique's last name. Maybe it was the real one.

Too late now. As Raider got to his feet, he heard a cry from outside. "Hey!" a voice shouted. "Look what I found!"

Raider ran outside. One of the Pinkertons was standing about twenty yards from the house, pointing down at the ground. Raider ran up to him. "Look," the man said. "Tracks."

Sure enough there were tracks of boot heels leading away from the house. Backtracking quickly, Raider saw where someone had slipped out the house's rear window, then crawled along the ground for a while, until he'd had the confidence to stand up.

Hill. It had to be Hill. Raider followed the tracks. They petered out from time to time, where he'd crossed hard ground, but about two hundred yards from the house, Raider reached a point where the boot tracks intercepted the tracks of a horse. Probably a horse whose rider had been shot early in the fight. The boot-and-hoofprints intermingled for a moment, as if a man had been struggling to mount a frightened or reluctant animal. Then only the hoof tracks led away to the west.

Hill. He must have slipped out of the house before Jones

had completely closed the ring around the ranch yard. It would have to have been just after dark, as the moon was getting ready to rise. Hours ago!

Hill had left his wounded man behind as easily as he'd left the others. The son of a bitch was free again. He'd slipped out of another trap. But where the hell was he heading?

Raider ran to his horse, mounted, then followed the horse tracks to the west. He was aware of someone behind him. He turned in the saddle. It was Major Bell. Together, the two men followed the tracks, but they only led west for a mile or so. Then they doubled back, passing well to the south of the house, but clearly heading for Los Angeles.

Raider and Major Bell reached Los Angeles a little after ten in the morning. How the hell were they going to find Hill? He could have slipped out of town by now, or holed up with someone.

Raider had a sudden idea. "Boats!" he burst out, turning to face Bell. "Are there any boats heading south from here, toward Latin America?"

"Why, yes," Bell replied. "The Pacific Mail Steamship Company. It has boats that sail to Panama. As a matter of fact, there should be one leaving today—"

Panama! The word thundered into Raider's ears. "Where?" he demanded. "Where does it leave from?"

"Why, the harbor. Wilmington. There's a railroad that runs out that way."

Raider had Bell take him to the station of the San Pedro Railroad Company. A clerk told Raider and Bell that the train had left over an hour before, heading for the docks. Raider quickly described Hill. "Why, yes," the ticket clerk replied. "There was a man like that. I remember his baggage. Heavy as hell. And he sure looked like he was in a hurry; worked up a real sweat while he was waiting for the train."

Hill. It had to be Hill. Carrying the gold Zeke had seen him dig up. "When's the next train?" Raider demanded.

"Why, this afternoon."

"Too late," Bell said. "The Panama boat leaves before noon."

Raider spun around to face Bell. "How far is is to Wilmington?" he asked.

"Twenty-some miles," Bell replied. "We—"

But Raider was already running toward his horse. Mounting, he raced the animal along the railroad tracks. The tracks led him out of town, south. He was vaguely aware of Major Bell, pounding along somewhere behind him. Several miles out of town, he looked back. Bell was half a mile behind. Doesn't want to kill that fine horse of his, Raider thought. Don't want to kill mine either, but I may have to.

The rails stretched on and on. After several miles, a train came into view, heading back toward Los Angeles. Raider paid it no attention.

Eventually he could smell the sea, somewhere ahead. He continued to follow the rails. Buildings lay ahead, then a pier. His horse was faltering now, blowing hard, beginning to shake. Raider stopped the shuddering animal. He dragged his Winchester from its saddle scabbard as he dismounted.

He ran the rest of the way on foot. His boot heels pounded loudly onto the wooden pier. But even as he continued running, he knew he was too late. Far in the distance, out at sea, he could see a patch of white, with a smear of smoke above it. The boat to Panama had already sailed.

CHAPTER FIFTEEN

Raider stood at the rail, watching the barren coastline of Baja California slowly slip by. It had been nearly a month since he'd stood at Wilmington pier and watched Benjamin Hill sail away to safety. The United States Steamship Company had few sailings to Panama.

"It used to be different," Major Bell had told him, a few days before the ship sailed. "There were ships to and from Panama all the time. Traveling over the isthmus was the quickest way to get from the East Coast to California."

Bell shook his head. "But now that we have our own transcontinental railway, there really isn't much need. Hell, it only takes a few days to cross the whole continent. And not too many people want to go to Panama just for the fun of it. It's not that kind of place."

While waiting for the next ship, Raider had done his homework. Panama was a province of New Granada, which some people called Colombia. It had always been a transshipment point. It was a natural route between the Pacific and Atlantic. The Panama peninsula dividing the two oceans, was only about fifty or sixty miles wide. Centuries before, the Spanish had shipped their South American gold, looted from the Incas, via Panama.

However, it was not an easy route. Twenty years before, during the great forty-niner gold rush, when hundreds of thousands had crossed the isthmus, intent on reaching the California Eldorado as quickly as possible, fever, snakes, heat, and bandits had claimed the lives of many Yankee and European travelers. However, until Vanderbilt had opened the route through Nicaragua, the only other routes from the East Coast to California were to either sail around the tip of South America or cross the prairies by horse or on foot. Both these routes took months, instead of weeks. And time was of the essence. The hordes of treasure-mad travelers were in a hurry to reach California before all the gold was gone.

Raider was in a hurry, too. Hill had nearly a month's lead. He could be anywhere. Raider's only hope was that Hill, as before, would believe himself safe, and grow careless. Hill, Gates, Wilson, Don Enrique—how many other names did the man have?

Thank God for steam. Before the coming of the steamship, traveling between the Pacific coast of Latin America and California had been agonizingly slow. Sometimes, because of the prevailing winds, sailing ships trying to reach California from Mexico or Central America had to bear west as far as the Hawaiian Islands before finally tacking back toward the California coast. Now, with steam, ships were no longer at the mercy of fickle winds.

Raider's boat made several stops in Mexico and Central America. At each stop Raider went ashore, carrying pictures of Hill. He'd had a lot of copies made of the original photograph. At each stop Hill was remembered; the man's arrogance drew attention. But at each stop he had sailed on, father south.

The weather grew warmer and warmer. One day, with the boat lying off a beach in southern Mexico, Raider leaned against the rail, lazily studying the lush green, palm-studded shore. Brilliantly colored birds were creating a terrific racket. It was a beautiful, if rather savage-looking place.

Another passenger, a man of about sixty, named Jackson,

joined Raider at the rail. "First time down here?" he asked.

Raider grunted. Jackson was a talker, and he didn't want to encourage him. But his reticence was wasted; Jackson needed no encouragement. "I first came this way back in fifty-two," Jackson said. "Heading from New York to the gold fields. Now, that was a trip. There was no railroad in Panama then, no docks on the east coast, nothing but straw shacks. On the Atlantic side, ships couldn't get any closer to the land than half a mile. We had to come ashore in little dugout boats the Panamanians called bongos. The natives would just paddle you straight in through the surf. If you capsized, you were shark bait."

Raider was about to tip his hat and find someplace else to stand, but he realized that anything he could learn about Panama might help him find Hill. If Hill really was in Panama. "What then?" he asked, encouragingly. "What happened after you got ashore?"

Jackson's face lighted up when he realized he had a real conversation going, a conversation that would obviously let him do most of the talking. "More bongos," he said. "Up the Chagres River by bongo, with native paddlers. Oh, wasn't that a trip! Jungle all the way, with animals screaming at night fit to kill. Which is what I guess they were doing. Or getting killed. And the boatmen used to sing these strange, monotonous songs. Like to drove you crazy. They were always trying to cheat you. Had to pay 'em a fortune to keep 'em smiling. And the contractors who arranged the trip—crooked as a dog's hind leg, every one of 'em. Those boatmen—all the people down there in Panama—you had to keep your eyes on everything you owned, or they'd steal it. I swear, they could steal the very cushion you were sitting on. Steal it right out from under your butt.

"The trip up the Chagres took about two days. We'd stop at night at these primitive inns. Ate the most curious food. Tortillas, tamales, not like the Mexican ones at all. Kind of tasteless. No chili. Then, when we got to a place called Gorgona, we had to switch to mules, for the last twenty-eight miles into Panama City. Meanest mules ever spawned. Some argonauts—that's what we were called back then, argonauts—

couldn't handle the mules, and got themselves carried that last twenty-eight miles on the backs of porters. Called themselves *estriveros*, those porters. Strong little bastards, never seemed to tire. The traveler sat up behind, on the *estrivero's* back, on a flat board called a *tabillo*, which was attached to the porter's forehead by a tumpline. Tried it once myself. God, but that board was hard!''

Jackson's eyes filmed a little, as if he had lost himself staring into the past. Raider verbally nudged him. ''I suppose it's a lot easier now.''

''Huh? Oh, yeah. They built a railroad all the way across the isthmus, back in fifty-five. Bunch of Americans led by a man named Aspinwall. They lost a hell of a lot of men, building that railroad. Lost 'em to snakes, fever, heat stroke. Drink, too. That killed as many of us gringos as all the other causes put together. Believe me, the tropics is the white man's grave. Anyhow, they had to bring in Jamaican blacks to finish the job. The blacks could take the heat and fevers better. Aspinwall and his backers ended up with the richest short line in the world. Terribly high fares. Charged twenty-five dollars per passenger, one way. I think it was forty dollars for a horse, but a hog could make the trip for a dollar or two. Worth it, every penny. What used to be a four-day trip through hell, took only four hours on the train. Still through hell, of course, but you spent less time smack dab in the middle of it.''

''Richest short line in the world?'' Raider asked.

''Well, it was. Until they built the Union Pacific. Before that, everything had to come either across Central America, or by ship, around the horn. Amazing what they did with that Panama rail line. They had interlocking directorates with the steamship lines. Could ship anything. Wells Fargo used to ship butter all the way from Vermont to California. Got there in fine shape, hundreds of firkins of it at a time.''

Jackson looked off into space. ''Golden butter heading west, gold dust heading back east, from the California mines. For a while, every thief and killer in the world was busy in Panama. Stealing gold, not butter. Until Ran Runnels put a stop to it.''

Raider nodded. He'd heard of Runnels. What he hadn't known, Major Bell had filled in for him. Bell, who'd spent quite a bit of time in Central America, had told Raider how lawless the place had been when he'd first seen it. For a while, the only way to get across Panama alive was to travel in well-armed groups. Bandits, killers, and thieves abounded. After the railroad was built, the line began losing heavily to these same bandits. "It was Wells Fargo that finally put a stop to it," Bell had told Raider. "The Hurtado Brothers, they were the Wells Fargo agents in Panama, they got together, with the Panama government, and hired themselves a gunman from Texas. Randolph Runnels. He was just a little squirt, maybe a hundred thirty-five pounds, wringing wet. Had a face like a choirboy. He was only twenty-two or twenty-three, but looked nineteen. We never saw him shave. Well, he came in as quiet as a mouse, and hired himself a bunch of spies. Black men, white men, Latins, he paid them well, paid them Wells Fargo money, and they fanned out into the countryside for a few weeks, just looking and listening, trying to find out who was doing the robbing and killing. And it worked. Wells Fargo had got the local government to agree that Runnels could do whatever was necessary to stop the robbing. He'd be judge, jury, and executioner. So when Runnels had the information, when he knew who the bandits were, he and his men went out one night, and collared them all. Quietly. Next morning, the old walls that run around Panama City were decorated with dozens of dead men. All of 'em just hanging there, by the neck. And damned if some of 'em were not important Panama residents. Big men, who'd got just a little too big, a little too greedy.

"Well, the robberies stopped right away. But just for a few weeks. Then the ones who hadn't been caught in the first sweep got bold again, and started their old game of robbing and killing. So Runnels bided his time, got more names, and struck back. This time it was the Panama pier. There were men hanging from its supports like mackerel. After that, I think a man could have walked the track all the way from Colon to Panama City, unarmed, carrying a fortune in gold, and nobody would have bothered him. The few of those owlhoots who survived, well, they took off for other parts."

At this point, Major Bell had grimaced. "Too damned many

of 'em came up here, to California. Caused us a lot of grief, until we started hanging 'em, too.''

Between Major Bell and Jackson, Raider had by now built up a picture of Panama as a rough place, an area that the gold rush had shoved into a prominent position way before it was ready. But the gold rush was long over, and the new transcontinental Union Pacific had taken away Panama's importance as a point of passage between the east and the west coasts of the United States. What would it be like now?

Raider turned toward Jackson. He appeared to be quite prosperous. "I suppose you struck it rich in the mines," Raider said.

Jackson looked at him with some amusement. "In a manner of speaking," he replied, chuckling. "I opened a hardware store. Sold picks and shovels to the miners. Made a fortune, while most of those poor devils went broke."

Eventually, in the middle of one fine morning, the ship reached Panama. The sky was cloudless, although Jackson promised Raider that it would be training by afternoon. "Rainy season," the old man said. "Rains like hell every day."

But it was not raining now. The sun sparkled off incredibly blue water. Ashore, the land was flat, green, and hot, with mountains in the distance. Even aboard ship, the heat wrapped around Raider like a steaming cloak. Damned if it wasn't nearly as hot as Houston in the summertime. Only the sea breeze gave any relief.

Once ashore, he immediately struck pay dirt when he began showing Hill's picture at the dock. Yes, they had seen a man like that go ashore. No, he had not gone back aboard the ship nor any other ship that they knew of. Aaaaiyyy, how could they forget him? Such an arrogant man. And his eyes, señor. The eyes of a corpse.

Raider felt a stirring of excitement. There was a good chance, then, that Hill was still in Panama. But how to go about finding him?

The city itself was small, a collection of tin- or tile-roofed wooden houses, with balconies for trapping the evening breeze.

There were not many places to hide. But would Hill be stupid enough to stay in town?

Raider checked into a small hotel. Now, problems arose. He'd had no trouble getting his rifles ashore, although he was pretty sure that the local law would frown on him carting them around town. They'd probably even object to his pistols, yet he didn't want to be unarmed. However, concealing a pistol on one's person, in a place as hot as Panama City, would not be easy. Damned if he'd wear a coat.

Raider eventually took his short-barreled Sheriff's Special from his valise and stuck it into his waistband under his shirt, which he wore outside his pants. Hard to get at, but hard to see, too.

Then he began canvassing the town, showing Hill's old picture again and again. He even left copies of the picture in some of the bars and restaurants.

He struck more pay dirt on the second day. The clerk in one of the larger hotels studied the picture, then looked up at Raider out of crafty eyes. "Well, señor," the clerk said, holding the picture up in front of his face. "Perhaps it looks a little like a man who was here nearly a month ago. Perhaps."

"Really? What do you remember about him?"

Another sly look. "He took one of our biggest and most expensive rooms, señor. He was a very generous man."

Deadpan, Raider slipped a silver dollar onto the counter. "Keep remembering," he said dryly.

The clerk pocketed the dollar. "He was here for a few days. He said that his name was Smith."

"Uh-huh. And where did he go?"

The clerk was looking sly again. Raider started to reach into his pocket for another dollar, but the clerk, after looking Raider over a little more carefully, decided it would be too dangerous to try to sell this man information he did not have. "I'm afraid I do not know, señor. He left with some men. They took his baggage away in a wagon."

"And the men?"

The clerk shrugged. "Señor, I did not recognize them. They were strangers."

The clerk clearly knew no more. Raider spent the next two

days not only showing photographs, but also asking after an American named Smith—if Hill had not changed the name by now. He got nowhere. Hill seemed to have disappeared completely.

After a week of fruitless searching, Raider had mined the entire town for information. As a last resort, he considered going to the local law, which in this part of Colombia, meant the army, but he hesitated. He had no legal standing in Panama. The locals might resent a foreigner hunting a man in their own backyard.

Yet, what choice did he have? He was still considering the problem one evening, as he stepped out of his hotel into the steamy heat of the street. It was the town's main street. The railroad tracks ran right down the center of the street. An engine sat, chuffing steam, about thirty yards away. It was probably the noise of the engine that kept him from hearing the sound of boot heels. A moment later, a squad of soldiers came around the rear of the train. The soldiers stopped about twenty yards away, facing Raider. "Señor!" a sergeant called out to him.

Raider hesitated. As if the hesitation was a signal, the sergeant spoke to his men, and half a dozen rifle barrels rose, pointing straight at Raider's chest. "You will come with us, señor," the sergeant said grimly.

CHAPTER SIXTEEN

For an instant, Raider thought of resisting, until he looked into the eyes of the men whose rifles were pointed at his chest. They were vacant eyes, eyes without feeling, the eyes of illiterate Colombian peasants, men from one of the most brutal countries on the face of the earth. Men who had been brought up in a sea of blood. Men who would kill him with no compunction whatsoever. "You lead the way, sergeant," Raider said quietly.

The sergeant nodded, then jerked his head in the direction he wanted Raider to move. He was a short, thickset, brutal-looking man, only a little more intelligent than his soldiers. He marched a step behind Raider, his right hand on a holstered pistol. The rest of the squad marched several steps farther back, their rifles still ready.

Raider was taken directly to military headquarters. At the door, the squad was left behind. The sergeant waved Raider in through the doorway. Isn't he going to search me? Raider wondered. He could feel the hard metal of the short-barreled Colt digging into his stomach. But apparently the sergeant, not seeing a weapon, did not think to look for one. Or maybe he was simply positive that his prisoner would not be foolish enough to try anything so desperate as to pull a gun in military headquarters.

Raider was led to a closed door. The sergeant knocked briskly. "*Mi capitán*," he called out. "The *yanqui* is here."

A voiced grunted a semi-intelligible order from the other side of the door. The sergeant opened the door and motioned for Raider to enter.

A slender man sat behind a desk. He was wearing the uniform and insignia of a captain. He was quite a dandy; his uniform was made of good cloth, and pressed to a knife edge. A narrow moustache lay flat against his upper lip. His hair was plastered down with some kind of grease, not a strand out of place. His eyes ruined the general effect. They showed a mixture of greed and stupidity.

Raider was told to stand in front of the desk. The sergeant went around Raider, to stand to one side of the desk. The captain leaned back in his chair, silently studying Raider. He said nothing, just looked. The little toad's trying to make me nervous, Raider realized.

It didn't work. Raider had faced down a lot scarier men than this dandified little captain. "Why the invitation?" Raider asked quietly. "Need someone t' play checkers with?"

The captain flushed. The sergeant took a half step forward, anger on his face. The captain held up his hand, holding the sergeant back. "You are arrogant, *yanqui*," the captain said. His voice was thin, affected. "You forget that you are not in your own land."

"I'm not forgettin' it at all. But I'd sure as hell like t' know why I been brought here. I don't like people pointin' guns at me."

"Silence!" the sergeant bellowed. The captain raised his hand again. "That's all right, sergeant."

Apparently deciding that his first approach hadn't gained him much, the captain now spoke directly. "I am Captain Gomez," he told Raider. "It is my job to maintain order here in Panama City. You have become a problem to that order, señor."

Raider raised his eyebrows. "In what way?" he asked, just as politely as the captain had spoken.

Gomez let a moment pass before answering. Steepling his fingers together on his desk, he said, "The questions you have been asking, señor. The photographs you have been showing everyone. You are hunting for a man, señor. What right do you have to do that in our country?"

"The man's a killer," Raider replied. "And a bandit. He's wanted by the law."

"In your country?"

"Yes."

Gomez looked down at his intertwined fingers, as if they contained his next question. "Then, señor," Gomez finally asked, "why did you not come to us first, instead of acting on your own?"

A good question, Raider realized. One for which he did not have any particularly good answers—other than a deep-seated distrust of any authorities he did not personally know. A distrust reinforced by what he saw in Captain Gomez. "I wanted t' find if he was here first. Then I would've come t' you."

Gomez nodded, looked down at his fingers again, then looked back up. "Ah, really, señor. You say you would have done that. But I suspect that you might have caused some harm to Señor Smith. Perhaps tried to take him back to your country by force, without considering our feelings in the matter. Without considering Colombian sovereignty."

This had, of course, been Raider's original intention. To do Hill a whole lot of harm. He was wondering how he would answer Gomez's last question, when he suddenly realized what the man had just said. "You mentioned Señor Smith by name," he said quickly. "You know where he is, then."

Gomez flushed slightly, aware of his slip. "Yes, señor, I do know where Señor Smith is. And I also know that he is a valued guest in my country. We do not allow strangers to come into our city and cause trouble for our guests. Do you understand?"

Raider nodded. Yes, he did understand. Hill, using the gold he'd dug up, had brought this foppish little bastard. "And if I brought you evidence of the crimes he's committed?" Raider asked. "The men, the women, even children that he's murdered, the people he's robbed—?"

For the first time, Gomez grew angry. "Enough, señor!" he shouted, jumping up from his chair, and slamming his hand down against the top of the desk. A pen rolled over the edge onto the floor.

"Enough," Gomez said again, but with more control this time. "I will not allow you to attack the name of a good man. Your slanders are not accepted here. I have been told by Señor Smith himself that the trouble that lies between you is personal. That it was trouble over a woman."

"Yes," Raider said, his voice hard and cold. "He murdered her."

"*Basta!*" Gomez snapped. "And if I were to tell you that Señor Smith claims that it was you who murdered this woman? If I were to tell you that it is you whom we would hang, if the crime had been committed here? I warn you. You are in danger, señor!"

Raider simply smiled, but said nothing.

"I am giving you fair warning," Gomez repeated angrily. He was having trouble controlling his voice. "You will leave Panama. By tomorrow. If not—"

Gomez let his threat trail away into ominous silence. Raider looked him straight in the eye. "I understand just what you're sayin', Gomez," he said coolly. "I understand ever'thin' 'bout you."

The sergeant strode forward. "You will address the captain by his title!" he said angrily.

Gomez waved his hand again. "Enough, sergeant. You can see that this *yanqui* is not a cultured man. Bad manners are to be expected."

He stared straight at Raider. "I suggest that you begin packing, señor," he said coldly.

Raider stared straight back at him. "I'll think 'bout it."

"Think hard."

The interview appeared to be over. Raider tested this hypothesis by turning and opening the door. No one stopped him from going out into the hallway. He turned and looked back into the office. Gomez had sat back down in his chair. The fingers of his right hand lay against his cheek. He was glaring at Raider over the top of the hand. The sergeant still stood next to the desk, rigidly, glaring even more malevolently.

Raider allowed himself a slight smile. "As I said," he murmured pleasantly enough. "I understand what it is you're doin'. I understand you completely."

He turned and walked toward the front door. No one stopped him, there were no cries of alarm from the office. He had not expected that there would be. About halfway through his session with Captain Gomez, Raider had realized that there was something odd about the Captain's manner. If Gomez had thought he could get rid of him that easily, he would have simply had his soldiers march him straight to the pier. Or lock him up until a convenient boat came along, then deport him. Gomez was hiding something. He was not totally sure of his power.

When he returned to his hotel, Raider made no move to begin packing. Instead, he lay on the bed, letting anger and excitement seep out of him. Gomez was a rodent. He'd sold his office to Hill for money. On the positive side, however, his conversation with Gomez had told him for sure that Hill was here. Somewhere.

The next day Raider changed tactics. Gomez obviously knew Hill's whereabouts. Therefore, it might pay to keep tabs on Gomez. There was not much point in physically following the man. Raider towered over most Panamanians; he'd be spotted immediately.

Instead, he roamed the dock area for a few hours until he found a man obviously down on his luck, a Panamanian with a look of hunger, a hard-looking man, one who appeared as if he'd do just about anything for money. "Would you like to make five dollars?" Raider asked the man bluntly.

The man's eyes widened. That much cash was a year's wages to a Panamanian. "Who do I have to kill?" he asked quickly.

"No one. Just follow a man. An army man. Captain Gomez."

Now the man's eyes narrowed. "That, señor, would cost seven dollars. Caskets are expensive, and I would like to be buried in style."

Raider handed the man two dollars. "You get the rest when you've followed Gomez until he leads you to another gringo." He described Hill. The man quickly slipped the two dollars into a pouch that hung at his belt, nodded, and walked away. Toward army headquarters, Raider hoped. More likely to a bar. In Panama, a man could buy a hell of a big drink for two dollars. The locals drank a vicious concoction called *aguardiente*, a vile, colorless liquid crudely distilled from sugarcane. It smelled like paint thinner. A few cents' worth would blow off the top of a man's head, with enough left over to embalm his corpse. However, later, after he sobered up, the man Raider had hired might start thinking about the other five dollars and start shadowing Gomez.

For another couple of days, Raider did little, showed Hill's picture a couple of times, but mostly just waited. On the evening of the third day, a timid knock sounded on Raider's door. Picking up his pistol, he went to the door. Standing to one side of the doorframe, he asked who it was.

"Señor, I have a message," a voice called out.

It sounded like the voice of a young boy. Raider hesitated, then opened the door a crack. Sure enough, a boy of perhaps ten or eleven was standing in front of his door, a ragged straw hat clutched in his hands. His face was anxious. Raider scanned the hallway behind the boy. There appeared to be no one else.

"Señor," the boy said, obviously scared to death. "A man told me to tell you that you are to meet him at the edge of town. He said to tell you that he is the man from the docks. The seven dollar man. He said you would know what that means."

Raider nodded at the boy. Well, it looked as if his two dollars had been well spent. "Wait a minute," he told the boy. He closed the door, then shoved the Sheriff's Special into his waistband, beneath his shirt. He was reaching for the door again, when he had another thought. Turning, he went over to his valise and pulled out his bowie knife. He stuck the sheathed knife into his belt, behind his back. In the nighttime a knife could be of more value than a gun.

The boy was still waiting in the hallway, hat in hands. He was so nervous that he was pulling pieces of straw out of the hat's brim. At that rate, his sorry headpiece was not going to last another ten minutes.

"Okay," Raider said to the boy. "You show me where the man is waiting."

He handed the boy a quarter. The boy's eyes bulged as he stared at the coin. For the moment, his hat was forgotten. "Sí, señor!" he replied enthusiastically.

Outside, the day was about over. It would be quite dark in another quarter of an hour. In these latitudes, the sun went down about five thirty. There was still enough light in the western sky for Raider to see where he was going. The moon was already up, and would soon be providing light, which made Raider feel a little better. He hated walking into a place he didn't know, especially in the dark.

The boy led him into a side street, heading for the back edge of town. Raider divided his attention between watching for possible trouble and avoiding the stinking pools that were scattered along the way.

This was a poor part of town. Because of the cooler evening air, the inhabitants were sitting in front of their houses, being social. Raider could hear them chattering away, until he drew near; the foreigner. Then silence would fall until he and the boy had passed by.

The street ended. A patch of bamboo, palm trees, and high grass lay ahead. The grass was about eight feet high, with thick, coarse stems. Deep shadows obscured the bamboo patch.

Raider realized that the boy had stopped. He was pointing toward the bamboo. "He said in there, señor," the boy said.

"Where? Cain't see a thing," Raider muttered, squinting into the dark shadows. He turned back toward the boy, only to find that he had disappeared.

Alarm bells triggered inside Raider's mind. He turned back toward the bamboo and grass, his body tense. And then he saw something. Saw a man in the growing darkness. But the man seemed to be floating in the air. How could that be?

Then Raider saw the rope around the man's neck. Saw that he was hanging from a palm tree. Saw that it was the man he had hired to follow Captain Gomez. And realized that he was quite dead.

A man stepped out from the bamboo into the fading light. It was the sergeant who had taken him to see Gomez. He was smiling, although it was not a friendly smile. The sergeant gestured to the hanged man. "A traitor's death, *yanqui*," the sergeant said harshly. "He died with your silver in his pocket."

The sergeant took a step forward. "You should have listened to the captain, *yanqui*. Because now you must die, too."

Raider searched the sergeant's hands for weapons. There was nothing immediately visible. Which suggested to Raider that he had not come alone. Forewarned, he was immediately aware of the soft sound of stealthy footsteps coming from behind him. He spun. Two men were approaching, only about ten feet away. Steel glinted in their hands. Knives.

The two men were grinning. They seemed in no hurry. Raider was not going to go anywhere, not with the sergeant behind him.

Raider held very still, studying his opponents. Both were small men; short, lithe, dark. They would probably be pretty fast. More importantly, they would think of themselves as fast. And maybe figure that a man as large as himself would be slow.

Raider considered reaching for the Sheriff's special. However, he'd have to pull up his shirt. And the gun would make a lot of noise, maybe attract the city guard. And he knew whom the guard would go for if they came running with their rifles.

The two men had spread out a little, coming at Raider from oblique angles. The one to Raider's left was a little closer than the other. He was the one who would attack first.

Raider let him come. He was pretty sure that the sergeant must have a gun hidden somewhere on him. If Raider made too much of a production of holding off these two, the sergeant would probably shoot him in the back.

The man to his left lunged at Raider, grinning as he stabbed his knife straight at Raider's belly. Raider pivoted to his left, at the same time reaching behind him for his bowie. It was a big knife, with a large, heavy blade almost a foot long. The edge was razor sharp.

Raider slashed down against the man's knife arm. The blade went right through his wrist. For a moment, the man did not seem to realize what had happened. He stared down at the stump where, only a moment before, his hand had been. He was apparently entranced by the blood spurting from the severed arteries.

Raider had no time to let the man stare. He struck with the bowie again, a backhanded blow to the neck, that nearly severed the man's head.

Raider moved quickly, shoving the dead man's slowly toppling body against the other assailant. The second man tried to move away from the blood that was jetting over him from his companion's neck; for just a second he was not paying much attention to Raider.

And then Raider was on him, thrusting with the bowie, ramming it into the man's stomach. The man grunted in shock. Raider withdrew the blade and struck again, this time into the man's chest. He felt the blade scrape against bone, and for a moment he was afraid that the knife would be trapped.

But it came free, with an audible sucking sound, and now Raider was whirling, toward where he had last seen the sergeant.

The sergeant was much closer now, only a dozen feet away. He'd been moving in close, to watch Raider die, but now his face showed shock; it was his own men who had done the dying. As Raider had expected, the sergeant had a gun, an old revolver, under his shirt. He was reaching for it now. Raider saw the man's hand settle around the butt. Raider thought of launching himself at the man, but he knew he'd never make it in time. The sergeant would shoot him before he'd made it halfway.

So Raider threw the bowie. He hated throwing knives, he knew that only fools throw their knife away. But he had no choice. He threw hard, hoping that even if the knife did not hit point first, it would slow the sergeant, hurt him. It was a heavy knife.

But it did hit point first. Raider watched it go into the sergeant's chest, almost up to the hilt. The sergeant had his pistol out by now, but the impact of the knife slamming into his chest threw him backward. His gun hand flew out to the side as he fought for balance.

Raider launched himself forward, seizing the sergeant's gun hand before he could recover. They stood face to face, with Raider's hand locked around the pistol's cylinder, so that it could not turn; there was no way the sergeant could cock the hammer. The sergeant stared at Raider for a moment, then looked down at the bright brass knife hilt protruding from his chest. "*Que puta*," he murmured once, then began to fall.

Raider let him go, taking the revolver from slackening fingers as the man went down. Raider tossed the revolver into the grass, then leaned forward to recover his knife. It was stuck into the man's sternum. Raider had to pound down with his heel to free it. He'd thought the sergeant was dead, but he screamed weakly as Raider pulled the knife free.

Raider leaned closer. The man's lips moved soundlessly, bubbling blood. Then his breath escaped in a rattling sigh, and Raider was sure he was finally dead.

He sighed. Okay, so he'd survived. But what the hell was he going to do now? He'd just killed three men, one of them Captain Gomez's personal aide. And there was the body of his own man, hanging from a palm tree. Gomez would now have an excuse to hang him.

Raider looked around desperately, but it was his ears that gave him inspiration. He could hear running water not far away. He pushed his way through the bamboo and grass. Fifty feet behind them, he came to a stream. It was pretty dark now, but he could tell that it was a powerful stream; it's waters rushed by noisily.

It took him another ten minutes to drag the bodies to the edge of the stream. He brought his informant last. He felt a moment's regret that the man wasn't going to be able to use that fancy coffin.

Raider rolled the bodies into the water one by one. He caught glimpses of them rolling away downstream. This little river couldn't be far from the ocean; the whole city was right next to the sea. If the water ran this hard and strong all the way, the bodies would probably wash out quite a distance. It might be days before they were found. They might not be found at all.

There was the boy, of course. He had taken Raider to this

place. But did he know Raider was to be killed? Would he even care what had happened?

Raider would have to chance it. He walked back to his hotel, moving quickly across the small lobby on his way to the stairs, avoiding everyone, just in case his clothes were bloody. He made it to his room undisturbed, then sat down to think.

Gomez was playing a rough game. There was no doubt in Raider's mind that the captain had sent his sergeant and the two knife men after him. He wondered if Hill had suggested it. Did it matter? When the sergeant failed to return and Raider showed up alive, Gomez would know that Raider had killed them. But he could not prove it. Would proof even matter here? Maybe proof was not necessary to hang a man.

Then Raider remembered Gomez's hesitancy, when he'd had Raider brought to his office. Something was holding the man back from openly disposing of Raider. He had no idea what that might be, but damned if he just wouldn't see if he could outwait the man.

He just hoped he was right, that there was something holding Gomez back. Otherwise—Well, maybe they'd give him a fancy coffin.

CHAPTER SEVENTEEN

For the next two days, Raider tried never to be alone, never to stand near a dark place, or an alley from which a hidden gunman might cut him down. He half-expected Gomez to send more killers. But none came. Nothing at all happened.

Until the third day. Raider had just left his hotel, and was heading for his favorite local restaurant, when his way was blocked by a man who stood directly in his path. The man's eyes were fastened intently on Raider's face.

Raider's hand drifted close to the butt of his hidden forty-five. But he hesitated. The man appeared to be a peasant, in his forties or fifties. His face was so weathered by time and the elements that it was difficult to guess his age. He was dressed in shapeless cotton garments and a ragged straw hat. He did not seem to be armed.

"Señor?" the man said, rather shyly.

Raider said nothing, but stood ready, his eyes flicking over the street, into doorways and alleys. Perhaps this man was a decoy, sent to hold him motionless while other men moved into position.

The man pulled something from the waistband of his floppy cotton trousers. He held it up for Raider to see. It was a battered, much handled picture of Benjamin Hill James Gates Wilson Smith. One of the pictures Raider had been handing out. "I have heard that you are looking for this man, señor," the peasant said.

Raider nodded his affirmation, his eyes still studying his surroundings.

"I know where he is, señor. I can show you the exact place."

Well, here we go again, Raider thought. Pretty clumsy of Gomez to try the same trick twice. First, there had been the boy, leading him into an ambush. Now this peasant. "Why don't you just tell me where he is," Raider said coolly. "I'll find the place myself."

Disappointment showed on the man's face. "You do not trust me," he said bluntly.

"Should I? Trustin' people 'round here is a good way t' git killed."

The peasant nodded. "Yes, señor. I can understand your feelings. Where Don Enrique is involved, there is always distrust, death, and suffering."

Raider's eyes snapped away from a suspicious alley mouth toward the peasant. "What did you say?" he demanded. "What was that name?"

The peasant looked confused. He held up the picture, pointing to Hill's image. "Don Enrique, señor. This man."

The name rang like a bell inside Raider's mind. Don Enrique. That was the name Hill's sidekick had used, as he lay dying inside the dynamite-shattered house near Los Angeles.

Raider took a closer look at the peasant's face, staring into his eyes. There seemed to be no guile there at all, only a little confusion—and something else. A burning intensity.

"Let's go back t' my room," Raider said, turning, and motioning for the man to follow him. The peasant, after a moment's hesitation, started after Raider. There was a little trouble inside the hotel; the manager was not about to allow such a ragged proletarian inside his establishment. "Get the fuck out of my way," Raider snarled to the officious little bastard. As an afterthought, he spun fifty cents toward the man, having learned by now that in these parts, money was the universal solvent.

Once inside his room, Raider had the peasant sit down in one of the chairs, while Raider sat opposite him, well away from the window, just in case there might be a rifleman outside. "Now, tell me ever'thin' you know," Raider said.

The peasant began hesitantly. Clearly, he was overwhelmed by his surroundings, which, while not exactly opulent, were comfortable. But once he began speaking, the subject matter galvanized him.

The peasant's name was Juan Olvera. He was, as Raider had suspected, a miserably poor farmer, from the country's interior. But he seemed to know Hill. He described him to Raider's satisfaction; Hill's coldness, the deadness of his eyes. "I will never forget him, señor," he said, his voice intense. "And when I saw his photograph, here in the city, after all these years—Aaiiiyyy! My blood turned cold. Then very hot."

Raider insisted that Juan start from the beginning. How had he seen the photograph?

Juan explained that he had a small plot of land about twenty miles outside the city, on which he grew vegetables. From time to time he came into town to sell his produce. "From twenty miles away?" Raider asked dubiously.

"I take the train, señor. It is very cheap if you ride outside."

He had come into town about a week ago. He described his surprise when he saw one of the photographs of Hill that Raider had tacked onto the wall of a cantina. He had instantly recognized the man as Don Enrique. He had not known, at the time, that Don Enrique was again in Panama. But only yesterday, he had caught sight of Don Enrique himself, riding with several other men. He'd followed them to a large house, where Don Enrique seemed to be living.

"Did they see you followin'?" Raider asked tensely. That's all he'd need; for Hill to get spooked again.

Juan smiled mirthlessly. "No one notices a poor old peasant, señor. He does not know that he was followed. Or even that he was recognized."

"How do you know this man?" Raider asked.

Juan's face grew bleak. "I have always been poor, señor.

But when I was younger, God saw fit to give me a young and beautiful wife, an Indian girl. She was a wonderful woman, señor. She was my life.''

Juan stopped speaking for a moment, his face working uncontrollably. "And then—one day—Don Enrique caught sight of her. He saw her beauty. He followed her home on his big horse. She was frightened, and ran the last way—to me. I ran out to meet her. Don Enrique rode right up to our little house. He offered me money for her, and when I grew angry, when I told him to go away, he shot me. Wounded me, señor. Left me for dead. Then—then he raped my wife. Raped her and raped her. And when he was finished, he killed her. Cut her throat. Cut her beautiful, kind throat.''

Juan seemed unable to go on. Raider did not push. Everything Juan had said fit in with what Raider had already learned about Hill. A cruel man. No, not just cruel. A man too devoid of normal feeling to be simply cruel. An evil man.

Raider stood up. "Let's go find this Don Enrique,'' he said gruffly, touched by Juan's evident emotion.

"Just you and I, señor?'' Juan asked.

"Just to see where he is. He has powerful protectors in Panama. We have to make plans, think about the best way to take him.''

Juan nodded bitterly. "Yes—he would have protectors.'' His face hardened. "But you intend to—how do you say it?— take him?''

"Kill him,'' Raider said flatly.

Juan nodded vigorously. "Good. I would never be able to kill him by myself.''

Raider thought of taking the train out of town. They would reach the area where Hill lived much more quickly. But if he took the train, if he went to the station and bought tickets, then boarded the train where it stopped, right in the middle of the main street, he would be seen leaving town, heading into the interior. He had little doubt Gomez was having him watched.

So he gave Juan some money, with instructions to buy two horses. They would meet that night, outside town.

Juan left. The rest of the day passed slowly for Raider. He went through the motions of eating, lounging, relaxing. He went back to his room a little before dark, as he'd been doing lately. An hour later he slipped out of the hotel's back door, dressed for the trail, lugging his Winchester and saddlebags.

To Raider's relief, Juan was waiting at the meeting place. Raider hid his dismay at the sorry condition of the two nags Juan had purchased. Well, they should be good for twenty miles.

Raider slung his saddlebags into place, mounted, and they were off, with Juan leading the way. Raider had to carry his rifle balanced across the saddle, such as it was. Locally, they used a saddle hard as a rock, and made for much smaller people. It was constructed of wood, part of it uncovered by leather. It was an incredibly uncomfortable contraption.

For the first several miles they rode alongside the train tracks. It was a beautiful night. The moon was out, and the air was warm without being stifling. Exotic, lush vegetation lay to each side of the right of way. From time to time they passed a big hacienda, set among fields of banana, corn, and sugarcane. There were other, smaller, much less pretentious dwellings, with walls of sticks, topped off by conical thatched roofs. From a distance they looked like big haystacks. These were the houses of the men and women who labored on the big plantations. The houses of the poor. Men like Juan.

When they had ridden about fifteen miles, Juan led the way onto a trail that meandered away from the train tracks. At first the going was easy, they were still in a cultivated area, but soon they reached heavy jungle. Although the road was apparently fairly well used, creepers had strung themselves across it in places. Raider marveled at the speed with which the Panamanian plant kingdom struggled to reclaim the whole damned place.

And then there was the animal kingdom. The ink-black jungle that pressed in tightly against the trail was full of screeches, howls, chittering, and murmurs. Only yards away a great hunting and killing was proceeding, as it had proceeded for aeons. Raider shivered.

About eleven o'clock, Juan turned off onto another trail, even smaller than the first. Half an hour later they rode into a small farmyard. Very small. A straw and stick hut with a thatched roof sat in the center of the yard. Chickens seemed to be roosting on the roof. The place looked very poor.

There was no sign of life. "Where the hell are we?" Raider asked. "Where is everyone?"

"They are afraid," Juan replied. "This is a hard land."

He called out softly. For a moment nothing happened, then a man came out of the hut's door. Raider saw that he held a naked machete in his right hand. The man peered at the two horsemen. "Juan? Can that be you?" he asked hesitantly. "On a horse?"

Raider could see the quick flash of Juan's grin, bright in the moonlight. "I have come up in the world, Pedro. Temporarily. But I have a favor to ask of you. Could you keep these two fine animals here for a few hours? Take care of them?"

Pedro nodded vigorously. Juan turned to Raider. "From here, we must go on foot. To ride too close—"

Pedro seemed overwhelmed when Raider gave him fifty cents for watching the horses. Juan was anxious to leave at once, but Raider made him wait while he rummaged in his saddlebags for his moccasins. There was no way he was going to hike through the jungle wearing high-heeled riding boots.

When Raider had the moccasins on, he caught sight of movement just inside the hut's doorway. He saw, vaguely, a woman standing there, with children on either side of her, watching, obviously apprehensive over the strange and frightening things happening in the yard.

Within another five minutes, Juan was leading Raider up a narrow path, through thick jungle. Raider had brought the Winchester and his binoculars. The rifle's barrel kept hanging up in vines and bushes. Once his binocular straps caught on a branch and nearly caused him to fall.

Juan had picked up a machete at Pedro's house. He used it now to cut through some of the denser growth. It was dark on the trail, with only a little moonlight trickling through the overhead canopy, but Raider was able to see the silvery arc of the machete as Juan swung it again and again. He could hear a slight ringing sound whenever the machete cut through something heavy enough to give a little resistance.

Their progress was very slow; it was almost as if the jungle was conspiring to hold them back. Finally, after two hours of inching along the jungle track, Juan stopped. Raider stumbled into him from behind. "Shhh," Juan warned him. "We must be very quiet now. We are close enough for them to hear us."

Now their pace became even slower. Juan could no longer use the machete; its sound might alert a guard. "And there are many guards, señor."

In places they had to crawl beneath vegetation that had overgrown the trail. It was warm in the jungle, and very humid. Sweat trickled down Raider's forehead. This close to the ground, he kept expecting to come face to face with some enormous poisonous serpent.

Finally, he could see moonlight again, straight ahead. He and Juan crawled to the edge of the jungle. Ahead of them lay fields of bananas and sugarcane, and beyond the fields, about two hundred yards away, a big three-storied hacienda. Juan nudged Raider. "That is it, señor. I followed Don Enrique to this house."

There was now nothing to do except wait for daylight. For more than two hours, Raider and Juan lay concealed just within the edge of the jungle. Bugs attacked them. Raider's face felt like a single giant swelling. Once, at least two large animals crashed through the jungle only a few yards away. Seconds later Raider heard a squeal of agony, then after that, a low, rumbling growl. Despite the sticky heat, he shivered.

Dawn finally arrived, a marvelous tropical dawn. A silvery light quickly grew. Everything looked flat at first, then the sun came up, its early-morning shadows giving definition to the landscape.

Now Raider could see the guards. He counted six in plain view. No telling how many others were out of sight. Every one of them was armed with a repeating rifle.

The big house began to wake up. Sleepy servants shuffled outside to collect firewood and haul water. Smoke began to rise from an outdoor kitchen.

The house's upper story had a wide balcony running around all four sides. At first only the lower floors were busy. Then Raider saw movement on the top floor balcony. A servant threw open a window, then went back inside. Raider studied the window with his binoculars. He could see very little of the room's interior.

He was so intent on the open window that he did not notice when another window, farther down the veranda opened, and a man stepped outside.

Juan nudged him. "There, señor," Juan hissed.

Raider swung his binoculars to the left, and focused on the man.

By God, he'd found him. It was Benjamin Hill.

CHAPTER EIGHTEEN

Raider spent the next ten minutes studying Hill through the binoculars. He watched Hill stretch himself awake, standing on his balcony, soaking up the early morning tropical sun. Raider felt a moment of hate twist his guts. He fought it down. Better to be filled with cold purpose than hate. The purpose being Hill's destruction.

For just a moment Raider considered taking his Winchester and seeing if he could hit Hill from where he lay. He immediately abandoned the idea. The range was over two hundred yards, a long shot for a .44–40. Even if he hit Hill, the guards would be all over him and Juan. Perhaps, if he'd brought the Sharps instead—

Idiocy. What counted was not simply bringing the man down, but living to tell about it. He nodded to Juan. "*Basta*," he said. "Enough."

They wriggled backward deeper into the jungle, until they were certain they were well enough hidden to stand erect. Then they worked their way back toward Pedro's place. The going was almost as rough as it had been the night before. In the daylight, with the difficulties of the trail clearly visible, Raider wondered how the hell they had ever managed to negotiate it in the dark.

They reclaimed their horses from Pedro, who was clearly a little in awe of Juan's new status as a *caballero*, a horseman. Raider and Juan started back to town. They did not say much until they had once again reached the railroad. Perhaps it was the greater openness of the landscape, the lack of jungle claustrophobia, but they began to talk. About Hill, of course.

"He was a very bad man," Juan said. "He was *jefe* of a group of bandidos, a very cruel gang. They robbed the people traveling from Chagres to Panama City. They robbed caravans, trains, even boats. They not only robbed, they killed, too—I think mostly for the fun of it. Cruel men, señor."

"And they got away with it?" Raider asked.

Juan shrugged. "For a while. Don Enrique, he had powerful friends in the city. Perhaps he shared with them some of the things that he stole. Many people knew who Don Enrique was, what he did, but they could not touch him."

Juan let a short silence pass. "Until the little gringo came."

Raider, half lost in his thoughts, almost let Juan's last statement pass unnoticed. Then he pricked up his ears. "Little gringo? What little gringo?"

Juan shrugged. "He was a small man, almost a boy. He came to Panama practically unnoticed, working for the rich men who owned the railroad and the shipping lines. He hid himself at first, working through hard men. Then, one day, when he knew who had been doing what, he struck. Men hung from the walls, señor, like bunches of bananas. Men hung from trees in the very jungle where we were yesterday. And some of those men were the *ricos* who had been protecting Don Enrique. And that is when Don Enrique learned fear. He disappeared from Panama, señor. At the time, I was recovering from the wound he gave me. I was waiting until I was strong enough to kill him, even if it meant my own death. But before I had fully recovered, he was gone. I thought he would be gone forever. But now—now there is another opportunity."

Runnels. The little gringo. Juan had to be talking about Ran Runnels and the manner in which he'd cleared Panama of bandits. He asked a few more questions, until he was certain it had been Runnels.

So Hill had been one of those men Major Bell had told him about: fleeing Runnels in Panama, running to California, to resume his bandit ways in a safer setting. Then later, running from California. Hill was known here, then. He had to be known by more men than only Juan.

He nudged his horse into a slightly quicker pace. Juan sensed his urgency. "What is it?" he asked.

"We're gonna see the Hurtado Brothers. They're the ones who brought the little gringo t' Panama. They may have some interestin' things t' tell us 'bout your Don Enrique."

Hurtado Brothers, S.A., was still the local agent for Wells Fargo, although the shipping business was only a shadow of what it had been before. Raider and Juan were courteously enough received in the Hurtado offices, but the first few people they talked to were young men, the new generation. They knew little about events of twenty years earlier. Still, they sensed Raider's intensity. "A moment, señor," one of the young men said. "Perhaps if you could speak to Don Eligio. He has been here since before God created apples."

The young man had exaggerated. Don Eligio was no more than seventy, and quite erect and alert; a dignified man, as only an elderly Latin gentleman can be dignified. He listened to what Raider had to say, nodding patiently But when Raider showed him the photo of James Gates, mother lode bandit, Don Eligio's eyebrows shot up. "Ah!" he burst out. "It is Henry Garnier!"

"Don Enrique," Juan added, nodding.

Don Eligio snorted derisively. "He does not deserve the title. The man was a cruel pig. But you say that he is here, in Panama?"

"About twenty-five miles outside the city," Raider said.

Don Eligio shook his head. "Amazing. Is the man insane? After he left, he was tried in absentia, and found guilty of many terrible crimes. He was sentenced to life in the mines. I wonder if he is aware of that?"

"If he is, I don't think he worries 'bout it too much. He has local protection."

Don Eligio's eyebrows shot up for the second time. "I find that hard to believe, señor. Who would be so foolish as to protect that monster?"

"An army captain. A man named Gomez."

"Ah. Gomez. That *gusanito*. That little worm. I've heard of him. What a fool."

"Yet," Raider said, "he has power."

Don Eligio laughed bitterly. "I know a man, señor, who has more power here in Panama than Gomez could ever dream of having. Come. I'll take you to him."

Don Eligio led Raider and Juan out into the street. They'd gone two blocks when Raider realized that Don Eligio was leading them straight toward military headquarters. He protested. "But Gomez has an office there."

Don Eligio smiled. "His is not the only office."

Don Eligio took them to a side door, where a guard was posted. A word from the old man was enough to have the guard let them inside. The guard saluted rigidly. Once inside the building, Don Eligio headed for a set of stairs, walking up them as if he owned the place. Maybe he did.

At the head of the stairs, Don Eligio led the way down a hallway. Raider could see more guards ahead, and he began to wonder if the old man was leading them into some kind of trap.

Don Eligio walked straight up to the guards. "Is he in? Is he alone?" he asked brusquely. One of the guards, a lieutenant, nodded deferentially, then went in through a door. He was back in less than a minute. "The general will see you now, señores," he said.

Don Eligio pushed past the lieutenant, motioning for Raider and Juan to follow. Juan seemed awed by his surroundings. Raider was uneasy.

Once again Raider saw an officer sitting behind a desk, but this time the officer was a general, and the desk was much larger. The entire room was large, with windows overlooking the harbor. "Hector," Don Eligio said to the general, smiling. He walked forward with his hand outstretched.

The general stood, smiling, took the hand. "Eligio—my old

friend. What brings you here, to this miserable den of bureaucrats?''

Now Don Eligio's manner grew solemn. He gestured toward Raider and Juan. "Old friend," he said to the general, "these men have news for you that will, I'm afraid, reopen old wounds. But it is also news that will interest you very much. Gentlemen," he said to Raider and Juan, "let me introduce you to Gen. Hector Torres, military governor of Panama. Now, Señor Raider, if you will kindly tell the general who it is that you have found hiding here."

Raider did. At the mention of Henry Garnier's name, the general turned very pale. He actually staggered backward a few steps, and sank down into his chair. "Garnier? Here?" his voice cracked. "Can it be?"

"There is more, Hector," Don Eligio cut in. "It appears that you have a traitor in your midst." He then told him about Gomez.

As he listened to Don Eligio, General Torres's pallor turned to an angry red. He abruptly got up and stalked to the door. Raider heard him having a low-voiced conversation with the lieutenant of the guard. The general came back into the room. Raider could hear feet marching away out in the hallway. The general sat down. "Now," he said to Raider and Juan, "suppose you tell me where Garnier is hiding."

Raider, with help from Juan, described the hacienda, and the route they had taken to get there. The general looked a little puzzled. Then Don Eligio got Raider to describe the house again. "Ah," Don Eligio explained. "That sounds like the old Sanabria place. It has been empty for some time."

Their conversation was interrupted by the sound of many booted feet outside in the hallway. A moment later the door opened. The lieutenant put his head in through the doorway. "He is here, *mi general*," he said stiffly.

The general made a motion with his hand. A moment later Captain Gomez was marched into the room, an armed guard on either side. He stared at the general, his face taut with worry. "*Mi general*," he said. "What is it I have done?"

Then he saw Raider, standing to one side, with Don Eligio and Juan. His face paled. He staggered, and seemed about to fall, but the guards moved in close on each side, propping him up. General Torres got up from behind his desk and walked over to Gomez. "You shame our country!" the general said. He reached out and tore the captain's insignia from Gomez's shoulders. For a long, tense moment he stared straight into the ex-captain's terror-stricken face. Torres turned back toward his desk. "Take him away," he said over his shoulder to the lieutenant.

After Gomez had been marched from the room, General Torres sat behind his desk for nearly a full minute, staring at nothing. Then he abruptly sat up straight, all business. "Well," he said, "time to plan."

He turned to Raider. "Do you know how to read a map, señor?"

Raider allowed as how he did. The general called out to the lieutenant, and within five minutes the general's big desk was covered with maps. Juan became more useful than Raider. Knowing the country well, he was able to suggest to the general the best ways of approaching the Sanabria planation.

Within half an hour, the basic plans had been laid. While the lieutenant rolled up the maps, the general turned to Raider. "We will start tonight. I suppose you want to be in on this."

Raider nodded. He pointed toward Juan. "Both of us. We both have reasons t' want t' see Garnier taken."

The general nodded slowly. "Yes," he said softly. "There are many men who would like to see the end of Henry Garnier."

When Raider, Don Eligio, and Juan left military headquarters, orders were flying every which way. Officers had already been sent in search of their troops. Raider turned to look back at military headquarters. "Busy little beehive, ain't it?" he said to Don Eligio. "Garnier's name sure stirred up General Torres."

Don Eligio nodded gravely. "Of course. Twenty years ago, the general had a son. A fine young man, his only son, Andres Torres. Andres had followed his father into the army. When the general was a major, his son was already a lieutenant. He had the makings of a fine soldier. The general was very proud of him."

Don Eligio was walking with his head down, his hands

clasped behind his back. "Then one day," he continued, "young Lieutenant Torres went out with some of his men to capture a noted bandit. However, someone in the city had betrayed the plan, and young Torres was ambushed. He was killed, along with most of his men. A survivor told the story of how the bandit chief shot Andres Torres in the face—after he'd been wounded and disarmed."

Don Eligio stopped walking, and turned to face Raider. "Do I need to tell you, señor, who that bandit chief was? Who the man was who murdered the general's only son?"

CHAPTER NINETEEN

Raider returned to his hotel to get a little sleep. Juan tapped on his door just as it was growing dark. "Time to go, señor."

Raider sat on the edge of his bed, blinking for a few seconds. He was tired, but almost immediately the prospect of going after Hill restored him. He got up, splashed water on his face, dressed, then armed himself. He took all his weapons: the Winchester, the Sharps, his Colt Peacemaker, and his bowie. When he walked out into the street, Juan blinked at all the armament.

A long train sat chuffing in the middle of the street. Troops were filing into passenger cars, rifles, knapsacks, and all. Horses were being loaded into boxcars. Toward the rear of the train, Raider saw a small cannon being lashed into place on a flatcar. "Goddamn," Raider muttered, impressed. "Loaded for bear."

He saw General Torres standing near the middle of the train, talking with a group of officers. Torres saw Raider at about the same time, and walked over to him. "You see, señor," the general said grimly, "that I am taking this seriously."

The general looked at Raider's weaponry. "I see that you are, too."

A cry came from the engine. Torres turned. "We're ready, Señor Raider. Come with me."

Raider got into the command car. It was packed with officers. It looked to him as if there was an officer for every two men. They all seemed excited, almost gay. He supposed they did not usually get much opportunity to do more than kill peasants. They were probably looking on this as heaven-sent training.

The train lurched into motion. Raider sat down at a table; the car was very well appointed. Many of the officers were drinking whiskey or brandy as they talked and gesticulated, each one laying out in detail just what kind of action he planned for his men. Raider wished Juan were here, to tell him more about the terrain, but there was no chance of Juan being admitted to the company of his betters, these shiny young officers, these sons of the wealthy.

An hour later, the train stopped at a small crossroads. Chaotically, more than half the troops were disembarked, along with a sizable number of horses for the officers. After much shouting and excitement, a ramp was fitted to the flatcar, and the little cannon was trundled down onto the ground, where it and its caisson were hitched to mule teams. Then the train left again with the rest of the troops.

It was a black night; the moon would not rise for half an hour. Everything was done by the smoky light of torches. It took another forty-five minutes to get the troops into ranks, and point them toward a rutted road that led in the general direction of the Sanabria hacienda, now Benjamin Hill's place. Raider wished he could ride out with a dozen good men, well-trained men. They'd hit the hacienda at dawn, when everyone was just waking up. Maybe they'd fire the place, drive the defenders out into the open, where they would have to surrender or die.

Then he remembered the way Hill was always slipping away, just when he seemed hopelessly trapped. Maybe it was a good thing that he was riding with a general, two hundred soldiers, and a cannon.

The moon was well up when they finally set out, a long

column of men winding along a jungle-bordered road. The little cannon bounced along near the middle of the column.

Raider had been given a horse, a damned fine animal. He rode for a while with the general and his officers, then, bored by vainglorious and rather nervous boasting, he fell back to ride alongside Juan. He had insisted that Juan be provided with a horse. "Well, what do you think, Juan?" he asked.

Juan wrinkled his nose. "They make a lot of noise, señor."

True, they did. Like most armies. And also, like most armies, they moved slowly. Hours dragged by. It was after two in the morning when Raider sensed excitement up at the head of the column. The horses of the officers were milling around in the middle of the road. The entire column ground to a halt, with bored, footsore men running into the men ahead of them. "Come on," Raider said to Juan.

Together, they cantered to the head of the column. "Ah," General Torres said to Raider, as he and Juan rode up. "What do you make of this, señor?"

Everyone was looking at the ground. Raider looked too. The ground was relatively soft at this point. He saw the marks of many hooves. "About twenty men," he said to the general. "Quite a few hours ago."

"How can you tell?" the general asked.

Instead of answering, Raider motioned for Juan to dismount with him. Together, they studied the tracks as best they could in the dim moonlight. Finally, Juan straightened up. "They are not from here," he said. "See, some of the horses have iron shoes. They are not the kind of horseshoes made anywhere near here. I would say that they are horses from Colombia. They passed by here late yesterday."

General Torres had heard. "Twenty men?" he said worriedly. "This road goes only to the Sanabria place. Why would they head there?"

"*Mi general*," Juan said humbly, packing his voice with all the humility necessary for a humble peasant to speak to a man of good family. "Perhaps Don Enrique is going back to his old ways. Perhaps he is forming another band of robbers."

"Reinforcements," the general muttered. Raider looked

down at the tracks. Now he was quite grateful that he was traveling with an army at his back.

They pushed on. By four, they were only a mile from the house. General Torres called his officers together. After he had issued orders, the officers went to their units and began to lead them away to the positions they would hold. Now Raider began to be impressed. With action imminent, the men moved cautiously, silently.

All units were in place by five o'clock. It was fully light now, although the sun had not yet risen. General Torres set up a command post on a small wooded rise about three hundred yards from the house. His troops were in place another hundred yards ahead, partially hidden in ditches and jungle. The cannon was wheeled into position another two hundred yards behind them.

Raider studied the house through his binoculars. It looked as peaceful as it had the previous morning. Had that been only twenty-four hours ago?

There were a large number of horses in a corral about a hundred yards from the house. The twenty mystery riders were obviously on the grounds somewhere. They must have arrived before dark the night before. They were probably sleeping somewhere inside the house; it was a large house.

Raider caught sight of movement on the far side of the house. His binoculars showed him troops moving into a patch of thick jungle. The rest of the troops had taken the train to another road, farther along the track, so that they could get around behind the house without having to pass it. General Torres had planned well; in another few minutes the house would be completely encircled. Hill was not going to slip out of this one.

By a quarter to six, General Torres was satisfied that everyone was in place. He looked over at Raider. "It is time to begin this little dance," he said grimly.

Below, the house was waking up, as it had done the morning before. Guards were being changed, servants were beginning their daily chores. Raider looked up at the window where Hill had appeared the day before. The shutters remained closed.

General Torres walked out into the open on his little hilltop. Raider wondered if he was simply going to order his troops to open fire. Instead, the general turned to face Raider. "We must make certain that he is there," Torres said, almost apologetically. "We must be certain that we are not attacking innocent people."

General Torres drew his sword. He faced to the rear, toward the little hill where the cannon had been positioned, then waved his sword over his head. Raider watched the lieutenant in command of the gun wave his own sword in return, then turn toward the gun, reaching down to tug on the lanyard. The gun jumped backward, belching a dense cloud of white smoke. A moment later the dull flat thud of the report reached Raider, just as the ball flew by over his head, giving off that peculiar "whup-whup-whup" howl that indicated the ball was not quite round.

The cannon ball flew well clear of the house; this first shot was merely an attention-getter. There was an immediate reaction from the house. Guards and servants froze in place. Others came running outside. Raider continued to stare at the third-floor veranda, at Hill's window. There was movement. The shutters flew open. A moment later Hill appeared, shirtless, holding the shutters wide, staring in amazement at the distant cannon, and at the troops half-hidden in the jungle, only a couple of hundred yards from his hideout.

Raider handed his binoculars to the general. "There he is," he said quietly, pointing toward the open window. General Torres put the binoculars to his eyes and looked up at Hill for a long, long time. When he finally lowered the binoculars, his face had formed into a rigid mask.

He handed Raider the binoculars, then turned back to face the house and Hill. "Enrique Garnier," the general called out, in a strong, carrying voice, "this is Gen. Hector Torres. You are surrounded, outnumbered. You will surrender immediately, or you will be killed."

Raider had the binoculars to his eyes again. He could almost make out the look of stunned surprise on Hill's face. Then Hill ducked back into the house, slamming the shutters. "He's gonna fight," Raider said to General Torres.

"What other choice does he have?" the general replied grimly. "If we take him alive—he knows what will happen."

The house became a scene of violent activity. Windows were

smashed as rifles were readied. Too bad, Raider thought, that Hill had an additional twenty men holded up inside what looked like a very strong building. If those twenty men had only been a day later—

Smoke began to blossom from the house's windows, as its defenders opened fire. General Torres issued a quiet order to a colonel, who passed it a little more loudly to a captain, who called out the order to various lieutenants, who shouted it to sergeants, who screamed it at their men. "Open fire!"

A hundred rifles bellowed ahead of Raider. The house's lower floors were adobe, the upper two were of wood. He saw chunks of adobe and wood splinters flying through the air across the entire front of the house. Not too many bullets hit close to the windows where the return fire was coming from. The night before, Raider had noticed that the troops carried single-shot muskets, some of them smooth-bore. They were not very accurate. The sharp cracking sound of the shots coming from the house, and the volume of fire, suggested to him that the men inside were armed with the latest repeating rifles.

The general was pacing back and forth on his little hill, apparently oblivious to the occasional bullet that whistled by. Then he tensed, looking past the house. "That fool!" Raider heard him cry out.

Raider looked past the house, to the patch of jungle where about seventy-five men were in place. Then he saw what had angered the general. A group of about twenty men, led by a young officer, had broken cover and were rushing the house.

"Glory-hunting young idiot," Raider muttered. He'd just bet that the captain leading the charge had never had much experience facing repeating rifles.

The captain learned the hard way. Raider could hear heavy firing coming from the other side of the house. Powder smoke climbed above the roof. The captain's men began to fall, half a dozen down at once, including the captain. The charge stalled, as if it had hit a brick wall. The men milled about for a moment, then turned and ran back toward the patch of jungle. Raider saw that they were disciplined enough to take their wounded with them, but two men were left behind, apparently dead.

General Torres looked disgusted. "There is no point," he

said to Raider, "in needlessly sacrificing lives to those animals."

He waved back toward the cannon again. Raider could see the officer in charge of the little gun almost jump for joy. He said something to his men, then jerked the lanyard. Once again there was a dull, heavy thump, making the air vibrate, and again the sound of the shot's passage overhead.

The ball went high, hitting the house near the roof peak. Tiles shattered, flying into the air, but there was little damage. Raider watched the gun crew madly reload. Then the officer crouched down behind his gun, sighting, while he lowered the elevation. Another shot followed.

This time the ball went straight through one of the windows on the upper balcony, shattering the shutters. A cheer rose from the troops.

After that, it became almost boring. Shot after shot tore into the upper part of the house, splintering wood, collapsing the roof, shattering windows. When the upper floor had been turned into a complete wreck, the gun crew began loading with grape, sweeping the open wreckage with hundreds of lead balls, like a giant shotgun. Then the officer in charge changed to canister. Raider saw an entire section of the rear wall fly away from the house. The gun's officer, knowing he probably wouldn't get another chance like this for some time, was experimenting with everything he had.

By now, anyone foolish enough to have remained on the upper floors must be either dead or dying. However there was still some firing coming from the windows on the lower floor. The gun lowered its aim. The destruction was a little slower this time, because of the adobe construction, but within half an hour, great gaps began to appear in the walls. And again the gunner changed to grape and canister.

Raider sensed someone standing by his side. He turned. It was Juan. He was staring at the house with something like pain showing on his face. He saw that Raider was watching him. He looked at Raider sheepishly. "This is all very good, señor. But I would much prefer to have my very own hands around Don Enrique's throat."

Raider knew how he felt. There was really not much to do.

By now the firing from the house had mostly died away. Raider saw the general give another order to the colonel, which was relayed in the same manner, eventually reaching the troops. It was an order to attack. Obviously, the troops had been getting just as bored. They ran forward eagerly, the bayonets on the ends of their rifles glittering in the bright midmorning sun. Their wild howl galvanized Raider into action. "Come on," he said to Juan. "We wanna make sure we get the bastard."

By the time Raider and Juan arrived, the troops were already surging into the house. He saw a man stagger out the door, waving a white flag tied to a gun barrel. Two of the soldiers, mad with killing lust, ran him through with their bayonets.

Raider pushed past the entangled trio into the house. A blood-maddened young peasant soldier turned and saw him. Eyes wide, mirroring the blankness of his mind, the soldier tried to bayonet Raider. Juan deflected the bayonet, then kicked the soldier in the groin.

The interior of the house was a shambles. Dead and dying men lay everywhere. Raider and Juan ran from body to body, looking for Hill. Each of them wanted to put his own bullet into his enemy's body.

But they could not find him. Perhaps he was still upstairs. The idea occurred to both men concurrently. Both rushed up what was left of the stairway. The upper stories were even more of a shambles. When they reached the second story, they saw that the third story had no floor. Hill/Garnier could not be up here.

They returned to the bottom floor, still looking. A terrible dread began to overtake Raider. Had the son of a bitch done it again? He remembered the times he'd thought he had Hill cornered, the times he'd been positive he had him. He remembered the house in Los Angeles, where Hill's body was nowhere to be found, simply because he had once again escaped.

The first blood-lust of the soldiers had diminished. They were actually taking prisoners, all of them wounded. Raider bent over a blood-soaked man. "Where is he?" he shouted, shaking the man, oblivious to the man's wounds. "Where is your *jefe*? Where is Hill?"

He corrected himself. "Don Enrique," he said. "Where is he?"

The man stared at Raider blank-eyed. He was clearly dying. Raider let him fall back.

He heard a sarcastic laugh from his left. He turned. A wounded man lay on the floor, holding his guts in with one hand. He was a very hard-looking man, probably one of the Colombian bandits who had arrived the night before. "He ran," the man said bitterly. "Ran like a rabbit, right down his hole. I tried to shoot the coward, but I missed. Ran right down his fucking hole."

"Down his hole?" Raider asked, uncomprehending.

"*Sí. El túnel*. His hole."

The man suddenly stiffened, then screamed, his hand clawing at his guts. Raider knew he was unlikely to get anything else out of him. *El túnel*. The tunnel. God, there must have been a bolt hole!

Raider began searching through the wreckage. Five minutes later, he found it, an opening in the dirt floor, half-covered with debris. He turned back toward Juan, then saw that General Torres had entered the house. "He got away," he said to Torres.

The general looked at the tunnel entrance. His face twisted with disappointment, which he quickly suppressed. He had just turned, to order some soldiers down into the tunnel, when Raider stopped him. "No," Raider said sharply. "I'll go."

The general started to say something, then decided not to. He nodded. A moment later, Raider was sliding down into the hole.

Almost immediately, the hole turned horizontal, running off toward the rear of the house. Raider could see nothing ahead of him, only blackness. He was suddenly aware of a light behind him. He turned. Juan was coming after him, carrying a kerosene lamp.

There was only room for one man at a time. Since Raider was in the lead, he took the lamp. He knew how vulnerable that made him, the only lighted object in the tunnel, but it was a lot better than groping along in the dark.

The tunnel was low and narrow, although it appeared to be

quite old. Probably built by the Sanabria family, years before.

It stretched on and on. A perfect bolt hole. Raider cursed, wondering where it came out. Probably far from the troops.

It was Juan who spotted the small excavation in one side of the tunnel's dirt wall. When he pointed it out, Raider held the lamp close. There were several small leather satchels sitting in the niche, half-hidden by pieces of cloth almost the same color as the dirt. Raider pulled the rags aside and peered into one of the satchels. The lamplight glinted off gold. Hill's booty.

Acting on instinct, Raider repositioned the cloth, then had Juan help him collapse some dirt down onto the satchels, hiding them. Then he and Juan continued down the tunnel, wondering if they would find Hill around the next bend, staring at them over a gunsight.

Instead, they saw a faint glow of light. The end of the tunnel. As they drew closer to the light, they grew even more cautious. Raider was the one who finally poked his head up into the open air, glancing around quickly to make sure he was not about to be shot.

Damned if they weren't smack dab in the middle of the little patch of jungle where the troops who had first rushed the house had been hidden. There was no one there now but the wounded. All the others must have joined the general assault on the house.

Raider climbed out of the tunnel. No sign of Hill. Raider was looking around wildly when a man lying on the ground called to him weakly. He was a lieutenant. He'd been shot through the chest. "Señor," he gasped. "You are looking for the man who came out of this hole?"

Raider nodded. The lieutenant swallowed once or twice, fighting for air. "He came up right in the middle of us. Only the wounded had been left behind. I had been hit in the leg. When I called out to him, he shot me again."

"Where the hell is he?" Raider demanded.

The lieutenant pointed toward a path that led out of the patch of jungle. "He went that way. My horse was back there. He tried to take it, señor, but he was too rough. He frightened the horse. It would not let him near. He tried for a long time, then he ran away. Ran down that trail."

Raider and Juan immediately started along the trail. Within twenty yards, they came out into the open. There was no cover for perhaps five hundred yards.

There he was! Raider saw a figure run into some brushy scrub at the far edge of the clearing. He had a hell of a lead.

Then Raider saw the horse, nervously cropping grass twenty yards away. Raider held very still for a moment, then began walking toward the animal. It edged away.

Juan came up behind Raider. "Let me," he said gruffly.

It took Juan only a minute or two of patient, soft-voiced coaxing to entice the animal near. Finally, he had it by the reins. He turned toward Raider, torment on his face. "You take it, señor," he said. "You ride very much better."

Raider immediately swung into the saddle. The horse trembled for a moment, then shot away when he kicked it with his heels.

Raider raced down on the patch of scrub where Hill had vanished. The bushes were about five feet high, easy for a mounted man to see over. He caught sight of movement, off to his right, the top of a man's head bobbing above the scrub.

Raider pushed his horse in that direction. Indeed, there was no other way he could go, he had to follow the trail. The scrub was too thick to be penetrated even by a man on foot. Obviously, someone had cut this trail.

At first, Hill did not seem to realize he was being followed; his pace was leisurely. Raider was only a couple of hundred yards behind Hill when the man finally turned and caught sight of him.

Hill began to run. Raider urged the horse forward more quickly, although he had to be careful; the ground was crisscrossed by roots; the horse might stumble and fall.

Ahead, the scrub ended in more open ground. A patch of thick jungle lay about a hundred yards on the other side of the clearing. Raider saw Hill break out into the open, running toward the jungle. For the first time, Raider realized that Hill was carrying something in his right hand. Something that caused him to lean a little to the left. It must be heavy.

Raider reached the open ground when Hill was still about

thirty yards from cover. Raider could run the horse now, so he let it have its head, racing after Hill.

Hill was running more and more slowly. Clearly, he was exhausted. Still, he should be able to reach the jungle before Raider caught up to him.

Raider raced the horse onward. Hill turned around the moment he reached cover. Raider saw Hill's right hand rise up. He had a pistol!

Raider lay close to the horse's neck. Hill fired three shots, Raider counted them. He heard the bullets whistle by him. Then Hill ducked onto a jungle trail.

Raider brought the horse to a sliding stop at the edge of the jungle. He slid from the animal's back, dodging into the cover of thick ferns just as Hill fired again.

The bullet came very close this time, but Raider did not bother to return the fire. He knew Hill was running scared, that he was tired, maybe even panic-stricken.

He heard a crashing ahead of him along the trail. Hill had started running again. "Run all you want, Hill," he called after the fugitive. "You're a dead man."

Raider began to lope along the trail, conserving his strength. He heard more crashing ahead of him. "I'm comin', Hill," Raider repeated. "I'm gonna kill you."

Another shot crashed out. Raider had no idea where the bullet went. Hill was clearly panicking. That had to be at least five shots. Raider nearly tripped over a small leather satchel that had been dropped in the middle of the trail. It matched the satchel he and Juan had found in the tunnel. Now Hill had nothing left. Raider picked up the bag and threw it into the jungle, out of sight.

Raider ran on, following the sounds of flight from ahead. He was so close now that he could actually hear Hill's ragged panting. Raider picked up a stick, and threw it ahead of him, into the jungle. Hill screamed an unintelligible oath, which was followed by the crash of another shot.

Raider zeroed in on the sound, running faster now. Suddenly, he came upon Hill, who had stopped at a wide spot in the trail. Hill was looking around him wildly, and now Raider realized why. There were shouts coming from every direction; it sounded as if the entire army was on Hill's trail.

Hill saw Raider. He raised his pistol, cranked back the hammer, then pulled the trigger. The hammer came down with a loud snap. The pistol, as Raider had hoped, was empty.

Hill snarled, and threw the pistol at Raider. Raider ducked, although the pistol bounced off his left arm. He kept coming. Hill turned and ran farther down the trail. Raider ran after him.

Raider could have drawn his pistol and killed the other man at any time. Instead, he ran him. Ran him like an animal, always on his heels, until he could hear Hill's tortured breath sucking noisily in and out of his mouth and nose. He ran him until Hill was barely staggering, until he finally fell against the trunk of an enormous tree.

Hill lay on the ground, staring up at Raider, who stood quietly about six feet away. From behind Raider, farther down the trail, the sounds of pursuit were growing steadily louder. Raider noticed that Hill's eyes were no longer expressionless; they were now filled with terror.

This was the moment. Raider drew his revolver, holding it loosely. "Remember Nanna?" Raider asked, almost casually.

The sound of Nanna's name seemed to stiffen Hill. "That bitch," he hissed. "She betrayed me."

Anger surged through Raider. He cocked the pistol. Oddly enough, the sound of the hammer clicking into place seemed to wash some of the terror from Hill's eyes. He glared back at Raider defiantly. Almost with pleasure.

The shouting of the soldiers from behind Raider was growing very loud. They would be here within a minute. And then Raider realized that it was the chase itself that had terrified Hill, more than the thought of death.

Raider pointed the pistol at Hill. Straight at his head, wanting to ruin the man's face. His finger tightened on the trigger. Hill was glaring at him.

Raider lowered his gun hand. Hill stared at him for several seconds, then he burst out, "Get it over with, for God's sake. Haven't you got the guts to shoot me?"

Raider lowered the hammer, then slipped the forty-five back

into its holster. "Uh-uh, Hill," he said softly. "I'm not gonna shoot you."

He smiled when he saw the look of relief on the other man's face. "I got a much better idea, Hill. Something that'll hurt a lot more'n a bullet. And last a hell of a lot longer."

CHAPTER TWENTY

Raider stood at the ship's rail, watching the land draw nearer. The heat was the same. So was the low coastline, the mountainous interior, the lush tropical flora. It had been a year since Raider had last landed at Panama City, but nothing appeared to have changed.

Except Juan, who met him on the dock. A much more prosperous-looking Juan, dressed, not in a suit, exactly, but in much finer clothes than he'd been wearing the first time Raider had met him.

The two men embraced on the dock, which made Raider a little uneasy; he was more comfortable shaking hands. Still, they had been through a lot together.

They wasted little time in Panama City. Juan hustled Raider aboard the train, and a few minutes later they were chuffing out of the city, heading east, up toward the mountains. Raider noticed that they were in the first-class coach. A waiter came over. Juan ordered brandy for both of them. "You will not recognize the place," Juan told Raider, as they sipped their drinks. "Why have you stayed away so long? You should come here for good, live with us."

Raider merely smiled. How could he explain to Juan that his life revolved around movement, change, travel? Juan was a man of the soil. Give him a few acres, and he was ready to settle down forever.

Although he now had more than just a few acres. A week after the assault on Hill's hideout, he and Juan had returned one night, equipped with lanterns and a mule. Descending into the tunnel, they had dug up the gold they had hidden, then transported it back to Juan's shack. Raider had insisted that Juan take most of the money. He kept only a couple thousand dollars for himself, enough to make this return trip, with enough left over for some additional travel. He knew that if he'd kept more of the gold, he'd have simply spent it. He'd never been able to hang onto money.

Juan, on the other hand, had invested it wisely. Raider could sense the other man's excitement as the train neared their destination. "The railroad has made a special station, just for me." Juan said proudly.

Sure enough, the train was stopping, right in front of a considerable collection of buildings, ranging in size from small houses, probably for the families of workmen, to quite large structures. "My God, Juan," Raider exclaimed. "It looks like a whole damned town!"

"It is. I've been building while you were gone. See over there? The really big one? That is the *posada*, the inn. People stop here now. I have the best cook in the whole country. And that other big building is the warehouse. We bring in goods from this entire area, then ship them all over the country. To other countries, too. I've set up a cooperative for the farmers."

Juan went on to detail his entrepreneurial activities. Confidence leaked from him. How changed he was from the shy, deferential peasant who had stopped Raider on the street a year before, to tell him that he knew where their common enemy was hiding.

They were met at the small train station by servants, who put Raider's baggage in a buggy. Then they drove to the inn, even though it was only a few hundred yards away. All three floors had wide, shady balconies. Juan took Raider up to the second floor, where they could look out over Juan's domain, while sipping cool drinks. "We have everything here," Juan said. "A blacksmith's shop; *tiendas*, stores, where people from miles around buy the things they need, from tools to clothing. I only go into that miserable city when I have to. Ah, but here I talk and talk, and you must be tired. Perhaps, you would like to go to your room."

"Whenever," Raider replied. True, he was tired, but it was so pleasant, sitting here on this shady balcony, looking out over Panama's lush greenness.

However, he could tell Juan had another surprise for him; he was almost bouncing up and down with eagerness. "Let us go, then," Juan burst out.

"Go? I thought we were already here."

"Hah!" Juan exclaimed. "This place? It is for whoever comes by. Not for those who belong. Come."

Raider was led down the stairs. He saw that his bags were still in the buggy. He and Juan got in with the baggage, and a moment later the driver had whipped the horses away from the inn, up a steep hill.

He saw the house when they came around the first bend. "My God, Juan," he burst out. "It's a palace!"

"Only my humble home," Juan replied quietly, but Raider could sense his pride. Why not? It was an imposing pile, a vast, sprawling house of three stories, surrounded by outbuildings. The grounds were park-like, and very well-tended. Servants met them at the front door. Raider's baggage immediately disappeared inside. Juan had mentioned rest, but obviously not until he showed Raider around. They toured the house, a combination of vast rooms and smaller, more intimate corners. Raider noticed that it was relatively cool. Built on a hill, the house picked up any stray breezes.

Juan took him to a high balcony at the rear of the house. They could see for miles. Miles of agricultural land. "It is all ours," Juan said proudly. "We grow bananas, chayotes, potatoes, fruit, beans, whatever will thrive here."

"Ours?" Raider asked. "Have you married?"

Juan shook his head. "I was married once. I will not marry

again. I mean that it is ours, yours and mine. It was you who
made all this possible.''

Raider was touched. And it was tempting. But what the hell
would he do with all this? He would become attached to it, it
would become a chain looped around his neck, nailing him to
things. No, this was Juan's domain. This was what he valued.
Still, to be able to come here whenever he wanted—

He said nothing, although he could feel Juan's eyes on him.
''Thank you, old friend,'' Raider said. ''But, as you said, I
am a little tired—''

''Oh, of course, forgive my foolish pride.''

He clapped his hands. A young woman, not more than six-
teen, appeared. ''This is Maria,'' Juan said. ''She will take
you to your room.''

Maria gave a little bow, smiling shyly. My God, but she's
lovely, Raider thought. Slender, but well built, with the biggest, softest eyes he'd ever seen. Careful, he warned himself.
Don't play around with the help.

Maria led him to a large, airy room at the rear of the house,
on the top floor. The room's windows looked out over all those
broad, planted acres. Probably a ploy of Juan's to make him
love the place. It sure was a pretty view.

So was Maria. She bustled around the room, fluffing up
pillows and putting his clothes away, all the while casting
fascinated glances his way.

There was a bathroom attached to the main room. To Raider's surprise, men began lugging buckets of hot water in through
the door and pouring them into a big enamel tub. Damned good
idea; his skin itched from the saltwater baths aboard ship. He
waited until Maria had left, then undressed, and walked into
the bathroom. As he sank down into the warm water, he sighed
with pleasure.

He was just getting relaxed, when he heard steps behind
him. He expected it to be another man with more hot water,
and he was turning to tell him that the water was plenty warm,
when he saw that it was Maria. He ducked down a little lower
into the water. He should have warned the girl that he was in
the tub. She'd be mortified.

But instead of running from the room, blushing, Maria

picked up a sponge and walked straight toward him. "What the—?"

"Your back, señor. I will wash it for you."

Mortified? The girl was smiling brightly. Well, when in Rome—

Raider leaned forward. Maria liberally soaped his back with the sponge. Then she moved around in front of him so that she could rinse the sponge. Her face was only inches from his own. My God, but her skin looked soft. And those wonderful eyes. She looked him straight in the face, smiling softly. Then she looked straight down the front of his body, and what she saw made her giggle and flush a little. Raider blushed too. The damned thing had a life of its own.

After she'd rinsed his back, Maria wanted Raider to get out of the tub so that she could dry him. He refused. There was no way he was going to stand up in this girl's presence. Not with the sudden swelling that was throbbing so strongly.

Looking a little disappointed, Maria left the bathroom. After he'd dried himself, Raider half-expected to find her in his bedroom, waiting with his clothes, but the room was empty. Disappointingly so. Raider dressed, then went downstairs. He found Juan in one of the small sitting rooms. "Ah—just in time for dinner," Juan said.

He led the way into a large dining room. Raider and Juan sat alone at a huge table. Servants began to bring in the food, which was very good; turtle soup, salad, beef, many strange vegetables, and wine. The wine was brought by Maria. She seemed unusually subdued. Raider wondered if he had somehow offended her, or if she was simply very nervous because of his swollen condition when she'd last seen him. When she went back into the kitchen, Raider said to Juan, as casually as he could. "A very pretty girl."

"Yes," Juan replied, smiling. "I thought you would like her. She thinks you are very handsome."

That was all Juan would say. Raider wanted very much to know if Juan had any relationship with the girl, but his friend would say nothing more. He and Raider had late drinks on the balcony. By then it was dark. Juan excused himself. "There is much to do tomorrow,'' he said. ''This place is a demanding mistress.''

Raider had no choice but to go to bed. It was warm in his room, but he carefully closed the shutters. He'd been warned that the only way to avoid fever in the tropics was to make certain that none of the poisonous night air got into a person's bedroom. Just as well; it'd keep out the demand mosquitoes, too.

It was dark as hell. Raider could see almost nothing. Good, because he needed sleep. He was just drifting off, when he got the impression that he was not alone in the room. He half sat up, listening intently. There! A sound near the corner. Goddamn! His pistol was still in his baggage!

He was reaching for the lamp, to use as a club, when a soft voice called out, ''Señor? I cannot see you in the dark.''

Raider hesitated. ''Maria?''

''Ah. Now I can hear you.''

The soft pad of bare feet. A moment later Maria was pulling the sheet from him. ''Is there room?'' she asked, somewhat breathlessly.

A moment later soft, silken flesh brushed against Raider as the girl slipped into bed beside him. She was completely naked. ''Yeah,'' he said huskily, as he felt the girl's firm breasts press against his arm. ''There's plenty o' room.''

A week later, Raider awoke, as usual, with Maria, Juan's special gift, sleeping beside him. It was quite warm; she'd thrown back the sheet. He rose up on one elbow, looking down at her. Uh-uh. Not just lovely, but beautiful. Her face looked so soft when she slept, so perfectly formed. Her body had all the perfection of youth. Taut, full breasts, with soft little nipples. His eyes moved lower. Velvety skin, a sleek, healthy body, with rounded hips and thighs. Perfect.

But he was restless. He got up and dressed. Maria woke up about halfway, smiled at him sleepily, then closed her eyes again. Good. Sometimes in the mornings she scared him; he was afraid she was trying to fuck him to death. God, how she loved sex!

He walked downstairs. He found Juan in the big salon. Ever

since Maria had first seduced him, Juan had grinned like a kid every time Raider came downstairs. But this morning, Juan was looking quite serious. "It is time," he said. "The boat leaves this afternoon."

Raider nodded. "I'll start packin'."

An hour later, they were at the railroad station; Raider, Juan, and four of his men, heavily armed. Raider looked at the men. "Do we need them?" he asked Juan.

"Of course," Juan replied gravely. "We are going to Colombia. Hell's living room."

The train took them to Colon, on the Caribbean. By late afternoon they were on a small coastal steamer. Late the next day they were approaching the Colombian coast. Raider saw huge fortifications: the old colonial city of Cartagena. The Spaniards had fortified the place more than three hundred years earlier. However, Raider knew that its massive walls had not deterred the English from taking it.

They slept on the boat that night. The next morning they went ashore. While Juan purchased horses and pack mules, Raider wandered around the old city. It was very beautiful, with narrow, winding streets, overhung by stone balconies. Nothing quite like it in the States.

In the early afternoon, one of the Panamanian guards came to find him. "It is time to ride, señor."

Juan's taste in horses had improved. Everyone in the party was mounted on a Colombian Paso Fino, meaning, in Spanish, fine stepper. And they did step very well; Raider's mount had the smoothest gait of any horse he'd ever ridden.

They rode straight out of the city, heading for distant mountains. Juan's four Panamanians rode with the butts of their rifles resting against their thighs, with each weapon loaded and ready. Raider had his two rifles, and his forty-five. Juan had a new Winchester. "You figure on trouble?" Raider asked.

Juan shrugged, repeating only, "This is Colombia, my friend."

They stopped for the night, making camp about half a mile from the trail, with their camp backed up against a sheer rock wall. There was only one way anyone could get at them, and that approach was watched by relays of guards all night long.

The next day they left the coastal plain behind and started up into the mountains. By the third day the increasing altitude had resulted in much cooler temperatures, although the terrain was still noticeably tropical, with vast, leafy forests.

On the morning of the third day they had just started out, when Raider thought he heard the sound of distant gunshots. Juan did not hear it, but one of the guards thought he had heard it, too.

They proceeded up the mountain. About ten o'clock, they saw movement ahead. Four heavily-armed men appeared around a curve. They were mounted, and were leading several pack animals.

Both groups stopped in place. It was only when Juan led his group about forty yards off the main trail that the others resumed their descent. As they passed, each group watched the other warily. Raider had never seen a more villainous-looking bunch. They were poorly dressed, riding sorry animals, which made him wonder all the more why they were leading such fine pack animals, with such heavy packs.

"Banditos," Juan said curtly, when the four men had disappeared from sight. "We will have to watch our back trail."

They continued on up the mountain. An hour later, they discovered that the shooting Raider had heard earlier had not been a figment of his imagination. Three bodies lay beside the trail, a man, a woman, and a boy of about thirteen. The two males had been shot, as had the woman, but she had obviously been raped first.

It took an hour to bury the bodies. When the last of the dirt had been scraped over them, Juan and Raider exchanged glances, looked back down the trail, then grimly nodded to one another.

They started back downhill. It was nearly dark when one of the guards reported smelling smoke. Following the direction of the breeze, they soon saw a campfire, about two hundred yards off the main trail.

All six men dismounted, then tied their horses to trees. Taking their rifles, they moved carefully through the heavy undergrowth. Within ten minutes, they were standing just outside a campsite, watching the four men who'd passed them earlier, sitting around their fire, drinking and laughing, while they pulled various objects from the stolen pack saddles.

Raider and the others fanned out a little, then simply walked right into the campsite. The four men did not notice them until they heard the sound of hammers being cocked. Four ugly faces looked up in shock. Then the six opened fire.

One of the bandits got his hands on his rifle, but never managed to get off a shot. A storm of rifle fire tore the four bandits to pieces. Juan and his four men kept firing even after the bandits were obviously dead. Bullets slammed the corpses this way and that, until the Panamanians' anger had finally been satisfied.

They left the bandits where they lay, with their stolen goods, they then rode up the trail again. However, it was growing dark. The danger of traveling at night forced them to make camp.

They reached the mines on the fourth day. These particular mines had been worked for a very long time, first by the Indians, then by the Spaniards, who had made slaves of the Indians to whom the mines had formerly belonged. They still used slaves, only now they called them prisoners, convicts.

The mine site was a vast stretch of blasted earth, littered with debris from generations of digging. All the surface wealth had long ago been used up. Now, the black mouths of mine shafts gaped in the sides of the mountain. Raider, Juan, and the others sat on a hill, watching long lines of shackled men move in and out of the mine entrances, like ants, bearing loads of ore-bearing dirt on their backs, which they dumped in huge piles.

When Raider, Juan, and the others finally rode down into the valley floor, the mine superintendent was at first hostile to their request. A Mexican gold piece quickly changed his mind. He turned Raider and Juan over to an overseer. "Do what they want," the superintendent told the overseer.

The overseer was a squat, brutish man, with a face that reminded Raider of the bandits they had killed. He growled and snarled when Juan told him what he wanted, until another gold piece changed hands. "All right," he said grudgingly. "He's over there."

Raider followed the overseer's pointing arm. At first he thought the man had made a mistake; all he could see were thin, scarecrow figures, staggering back and forth. Not the man he was looking for.

Then he saw that one of the men was indeed Benjamin Hill. "There," he told Juan.

Together, the two men walked toward Hill. He had just come from the mine entrance. He had a heavy basket of ore up on his back, staggering along under its weight. His work was made more difficult by the heavy chains that linked his ankles; he could only take short steps. Raider saw that the rings the chains were attached to had rubbed Hill's ankles raw. The wounds had festered. Raider was sure he could see maggots.

Hill was filthy, emaciated, barely able to stagger. Half-healed scars from whippings scored his back and flanks. His hands were dirty claws, ending in filthy, broken nails. He was barefoot.

Hill shambled on toward Raider and Juan, painfully putting one foot in front of the other. The overseer had come up beside Raider. "That one, he's weak. He will not last another year."

By now, Hill was only a few feet away. He hesitated when he saw the three men standing in front of him. His eyes showed fear when he saw the overseer. He started to cringe. Then he saw Raider and Juan.

He stood stock still, staring. For just a moment Raider looked right into Hill's eyes. At first, he saw only blankness in those well-remembered eyes, then perhaps a moment of recognition, a moment of hate and panic combined. Then the recognition faded again into a blankness that Raider realized was total madness.

Hill started walking again, staggering beneath his heavy load. The overseer, perhaps just to show Raider and Juan who was boss, snarled at Hill, then struck with the heavy whip he was carrying. Dust jumped from Hill's scarred hide, but otherwise, he did not seem to acknowledge the blows. So the overseer struck harder.

Raider seized the man's arm. "That's enough," he said sharply.

For a moment the overseer tried to meet Raider's gaze, but

his eyes faltered, and he walked away, grumbling. Raider knew he would probably take it out on Hill later.

He and Juan watched Hill shamble away. "So justice does exist, after all," Juan said softly.

Raider turned away, looking back down the mountain, over a huge vista that seemed to stretch down and away forever. Juan also turned away from Hill, and stood watching with Raider. But neither man was really seeing the stupendous view. Each was looking into his past, and each was seeing, in his mind, the woman whom the shambling wreck behind them had taken away forever.

"Yes—I suppose—justice."

A special offer for people who enjoy reading the best Westerns published today. If you enjoyed this book, subscribe now and get ...

TWO FREE WESTERNS!
A $5.90 VALUE—NO OBLIGATION

If you enjoyed this book and would like to read more of the very best Westerns being published today, you'll want to subscribe to True Value's Western Home Subscription Service. If you enjoyed the book you just read and want more of the most exciting, adventurous, action packed Westerns, subscribe now.

TWO FREE BOOKS

When you subscribe, we'll send you your first month's shipment of the newest and best 6 Westerns for you to preview. With your first shipment, two of these books will be yours as our introductory gift to you absolutely **FREE**, regardless of what you decide to do.

Special Subscriber Savings

As a True Value subscriber all regular monthly selections will be billed at the low subscriber price of just $2.45 each. That's at least a savings of $3.00 each month below the publishers price. There is never any shipping, handling or other hidden charges. What's more there is no minimum number of books you must buy, you may return any selection for full credit and you can cancel your subscription at any time. A TRUE VALUE!

Mail the coupon below

To start your subscription and receive 2 FREE WESTERNS, fill out the coupon below and mail it today. We'll send your first shipment which includes 2 FREE BOOKS as soon as we receive it.